T0170366

2013

ALSO BY N. NOSIRRAH

God Is an Atheist
Practical Obsession
Chronic Eros
Nothing from Nothing

2013

How to Profit from the Prophets in the Coming End of the World

N. NOSIRRAH

Illustrations by A. Nosirrah

First Sentient Publications edition 2010

A paperback original

Cover design by Kim Johansen, Black Dog Design
Book design by Timm Bryson
Illustrations by A. Nosirrah

Library of Congress Cataloging-in-Publication Data

Nosirrah, N. (Nevets)
2013 : how to profit from the prophets in the coming end of the world / N. Nosirrah. — 1st Sentient Publications ed.
p. cm.
ISBN 978-1-59181-095-7
1. End of the world—Fiction. 2. Experimental fiction. I. Title. II. Title: Twenty thirteen.
PS3614.O7835A614 2010
813'.6—dc22

2010002189

Printed in the United States of America

10 9 8 7 6 5 4 3 2 1

SENTIENT PUBLICATIONS
A Limited Liability Company
1113 Spruce Street
Boulder, CO 80302
www.sentientpublications.com

INTRODUCTION

For N. Nosirrah, the world we perceive is fiction. But, there's another, unseen world where truth resides, and in the spread between these worlds is the profit (and maybe a little transformation). In this powerful semi-autobiographical, tell-all, self-help, think-and-grow-rich, philosophical treatise and survivalist manual cum novella, Nosirrah explores the world monetary collapse and coming end times with his renowned though contradictory insights, unrelenting scatological wit, and multi-level marketing offer for readers of this book only. Have you ever awakened in the night wondering if you would survive the impact of a meteorite, a mutating viral pandemic turning the population into flesh eating zombies, the melting polar ice caps altering the climate into an inhospitable methane laced bog, or even God raining down fire and brimstone and turning off the lights on the way out? If you wake up screaming in the middle of the night with visions of Armageddon, or a loved one lying next to you does (or anyone on the cell block for that matter), then this is your essential guide to survival, prosperity and peace when the world ends.

N. Nosirrah resides in a vast but discontinuous universe where he writes fascinating cryptic novellas for a small, rabid following of readers old enough to know better but unable to help themselves or anyone else. I know him as a mystic, as perhaps the greatest writer of novellas of his generation and as a man, a man of insatiable sensuous appetites who has a PhD in Carnal Knowledge but never left kindergarten in Commitment. His idea of monogamy is that the universe is one, there is no separation, so why not jump in bed with every trollop that comes to his book signings or who listens in awe to his manic insights? Yes, they are young, slender and voluptuous, Nosirrah, but none has dedicated her entire life and every pound of her plus-sized body to your profound work except me. I toil to make your words shine like the gleam in your eyes as you gazed at me long ago at the all-night diner, passions finally exhausted after our "work out" at my loft, or so I thought. You were still hungry, and not just for the chili dog with Brussels sprouts and chocolate sauce you love so much, but for the woman sitting at the next table whom you invited to a tête-à-tête-à-tête back at the loft. There is no end to your love, you are not one for just a fling on the side but a ménage a thousand, and I could not share you like that anymore. You still need me, and I still long for you, but the cataclysmic gravity that attracts us and destroys us at the same time will be sublimated into our art, this art, the birthing of great literature for the good of the world. For you, the reader, you need not wonder about the passion lost, you will experience it in the pages of this work, which is about losing everything, for while love lost is the end of the world, nothing is truly lost, just converted in the end to a different but parallel universe and in that, a new beginning.

—LYDIA SMYTH,
Editor

2013

THE END.

The end of the world.

The end of you and all the history that comes before you.

I am writing this book in reverse order, starting at the end and ending in the beginning. This is how we think after all. Thought looks backwards in reflection to the beginning of each moment, and we could say that at the end of thought is the beginning of everything else.

But let me get to the final point of this book, which is more or less as follows:

Dear friends, the end of the world is coming and you need to be prepared. Now that you have read this book you may feel secure in understanding the end of the world, but I must tell you that this understanding will not help you. This book might have helped you, it might have prepared you, it might even have eased your fears, although I doubt that, but this book will most certainly not save you from the end of the world. The end of the world is coming and nothing can save you. The end of the world is now. That didn't hurt did it? Were you prepared? Not really. Were your fears eased by the end? Likely not. When the end comes, it comes, the show is over and there is nothing to reflect upon regarding that end, there is no need to worry about another end after that end, or to try to make the end the best end that you can have, because when the end comes it is over.

And, it really is over. Although, of course, you could stock up on canned food, just in case you survive the end of the world.

The problem is that the world is about to end again, there it goes. Did *that* hurt? No, it didn't and again you were unprepared and you are still not free of your fear. Here is the rub: the world is discontinuous, it is always ending, and the ending never hurts. That seems simple enough, and it may explain some things but it doesn't explain why we live in fear of the end times. Fear hurts, the end doesn't.

This is why I am beginning at the end and ending at the beginning. Fear spelled backwards is raef. If I insisted that you face your raef you might look at me quizzically, perhaps back away slightly, checking your distance to the nearest exit, fingering your cell phone in preparation for dialing 911 or your keychain where you have the little canister of pepper spray. I know this because I have tried this experiment all over the world, walking down the street and shouting "Raef" at anyone I met. Everyone acted as if I had asked them to experience fear, and so my friends, I am suggesting to you that forwards or backwards, fear is with you from the very end to the very beginning. Or vice versa, of course.

You will see that as we progress to the very first pages of this survival manual/novella, fear will be your constant companion. I will tell you how you can profit from the prophets of doom, how to make untold wealth for your retirement in the post-apocalyptic worlds, I will enumerate the dozens of ways that the world is likely to end, I will even make it clear to you that there is no way out for you or anyone else so that you don't spend any unnecessary time concerning yourself with escape. Remember, follow my advice and you will be rich beyond your wildest dreams, although when the world ends that won't mean a whole lot—you and your riches, and your wildest dreams, and my advice will be nothing at all.

And who am I to advise you on anything? I am the world's greatest expert on the end of the world, having come to the end of the world over and over and over. I am Nosirrah and my expertise is that I am not. My world is not. And, really, to be quite candid with you, you are not, and your world too. The arising of thought generates the illusion of self, and like all illusions, once one has seen behind the curtain, the illusion disappears and the actual is all that is left. Our collection of thoughts, descriptions and ideas is the stuff with which we construct the world, the world that is not, while the actual is made up of the silence that wraps around our noisy minds.

I live in the world that is not, as one who is not, so for me the world has come to an end, along with fear of that end, and I am left just with raef. Raef is the realization of temporal confusion, that is to say, time does not move just forward, gobbling the tasty future into the maw of the present, digesting and shitting out the past as waste, a toxic and foul realm that we face only with trepidation. Raef is random time, time without linear structure, time full of coincidence, synchronicity and magic, in which we can as easily live fast-forward or rewind or play, where pause is as available as eject/reset. Random access eliminates fear. RAEF. Freedom from the construct of time is freedom from fear if the future is the past, or more precisely, neither exists other than upon our arrival, our occurrence and our construction of that temporal reference. Then unless we create fear for the texture, tension and intensity that it adds to our created reality, we are free.

No time, no world. Game over. Game begins. Game over. Game begins. Get used to it. It is the end of the world, again. And again. You could start buying gold and silver, which would take care of you if the world ends because of sudden collapse of the global monetary system. You could use the gold to buy food, clothing, fuel and possibly guns. Although, in that scenario, the guy with the guns isn't likely to accept your gold for his guns when he can simply accept your gold by using his guns…on you. Remember, guns don't kill people, survivalists kill people when the world ends. But we are getting ahead of ourselves, which is easy to do when we start at the end, and getting ahead of ourselves when we are atemporal is just as easy as falling behind, holding still or just plain finding ourselves in an entirely different lifetime.

Like there was the time that I bumped my head on the counter top, you know where you are picking something up off the kitchen floor and you hit your head as you stand up and you see stars for a moment. By stars, I mean the celestial kind, not the red carpet kind, although Angelina Jolie fits both descriptions I suppose, and I would be happy to mediate her little dispute with Jennifer Aniston anytime. I have been told by my dermatologist my face looks a little like Brad Pitt, although on second thought maybe he said "bad pitting."

But back to the stars you see when you hit your head.

The next moment the stars subside slightly as I gaze up at the night sky in Australia, at least it seems like Australia, endless bleak dessert with scrub and nothing else and I realize that I have shifted into another time and place. It is a post-apocalyptic world in which humans kill each other for the scraps of food and the detritus of the industrialized world. Road warriors roar up and down the highways in search of gasoline to fill their empty tanks so that they can roar up and down the highways, and while this may sound like the life of a contemporary commuter, it is a parallel life of Nosirrah, soon to be known as Mad Nox, Road Pacifist. He was prepared for the end of the world as we know it, and he dutifully bought gold coins when everyone else was buying stock in big oil companies and those multinational conglomerates that always get those no-bid contracts to build the weapons to destroy cities in war, and then get the no-bid contracts to rebuild the same cities. Those stocks looked like good investments and, yes, there was a 20 percent return even after the brokerages, market makers and inside traders got their cuts. But what Mad Nox realized as he scraped his meager dollars together to buy American Eagle gold coins and a few Krugerrands for variety, when the global monetary system collapses, all those returns, all those stock shares, all those inside trades weren't going to mean diddly because all the investors would be holding was their electronic statements, at least until the electricity shut down for the last time and then they would be holding nada. Nosirrah would be holding gold.

Mad Nox, Road Pacifist

As the world system came off its wheels, the cities went to full time riots and the countryside to famine. The no-bid government security "contractors" destroyed but forgot to rebuild. Mad Nox calmly loaded his gold, his well worn copy of Gandhi's *The Story of My Experiments with Truth* and his highly trained Labradoodle into his Prius Hybrid Synergy Drive with Push Button Start and Solar Panel Sun Roof (50 mpg) and headed out to cruise the highways, confident in his survivability in a world gone crazy. I still remember the feeling of absolute freedom as I sped down the highway at a gas-consumption optimizing 55 miles per hour, windows rolled down slightly so as not to impact my mileage due to wind drag but enough so that the dry wind blew through my hair, not on my head of course, there isn't much hair there, but the feeling of wind blowing through your nostril hair is really the feeling of total freedom, don't you think? The world might be ending, but Mad Nox, Road Pacifist, was reborn.

Unfortunately, that sense of freedom didn't last long as I was soon surrounded by gas guzzling motorcycles, chopped down tow trucks and souped up pickup trucks with crossbows mounted on them. It was like a bad, low budget cult movie starring Mel Gibson, but damn it, it was *my* movie and I was going to make the best of it. I was doing the Mel Gibson part of Mad Max, and being concerned with global warming even though I was in a post-industrial world, I had replaced Mel's 1973 Ford Falcon XB GT coupe turbocharged Pursuit Special with my Hybrid (with Cruise Control!). But back to my movie, we stopped our vehicles and the gang leader was a big guy named Lord Hummus who demanded I give him my car or he and his boys would shoot me full of his nasty arrows. He had no idea who he was dealing with, after all I had taken not one, but two of the Marshal Rosenberg Non-violent Communication weekend seminars, and I was ready to help them meet their needs.

"Give me everything," Hummus grunted, articulating a need he was only beginning to understand.

"Hummus, I'm guessing you have unfulfilled needs and if we can just find how those needs can be met, we won't have any conflict, am I right?"

"Give me everything now, or you die!" Hummus bellowed.

"Well, I can certainly see that you are feeling mad," I said, using my NVC training, "and that makes me feel sad. You see, it is important that we acknowledge the simple emotions that we experience when our needs are not met and that we begin to speak them to each other. For example, when the world as we knew it came to an end, I certainly felt sad and mad, but not bad, because I knew that it wasn't my fault. I had replaced all my incandescent bulbs with compact fluorescent, I was composting my organic scraps and I drank only fair trade coffee. I was glad I didn't feel sad. I am guessing that you, Lord Hummus, feel bad, am I right?"

"Give me everything, *and* you die!" Hummus was livid, and had upped the ante. This told me that we were getting to the point of communication. I felt glad. At the same time it seemed like our Non-Violent Communication session might be better off if we rescheduled it for another movie.

"Hummus, I am not a violent man, how about if I give you a gold coin and you give me safe passage?"

"Give me everything, all your gold coins, you die *and* we torture you horribly first just for fun."

My Non-Violent Communication training seemed to be paying off after all, no need to reschedule. Hummus seemed to be connecting directly to his needs and was now expressing them. Unfortunately, as a psychopathic killer his needs were best fulfilled by staking me to a fire ant hill (this was a bad movie after all) and leaving me to expire in the sun after taking my car, my dog and all my gold. Note to self, in next dream sequence, hallucination, or parallel universe lifetime, bring weapons along with the gold and Non-Violent Communication tapes. Non-violence might not be well suited for a post-industrial, post-civilization world. Also, no sunscreen—fire ants seem to love it.

Days later, in the last wheezing moments of the life of Mad Nox, Road Pacifist, just as that world ended with the dying gasps through parched lips swollen with ant stings, the sun was so searing that my eyes were burned, I saw lights within lights within lights like a hundred sparklers, and standing upright, rubbed my head. Kitchen counters are hard and hitting your head on one hurts, but where one movie closes, another opens. I was back in my kitchen, Mad Nox a fading memory of a possible future now past. I was just Nosirrah, but what movie had I entered? What world did I now occupy? And almost before that question had formed in my still foggy mind, along came the companion question: whatever this world was, when would it come to an end and would I survive those end times?

There seem to be two categories of end-of-world scenarios. Type one is where the world meets a calamity that simply destroys it, it is over, period. The Blue Screen of Death, your computer will not reboot and your Windows operating system has had a complete meltdown and ceases to function. You can prepare for this end of the world by going off the grid, learning to hunt your own food, and studying basic survival skills so that when the world shuts down you won't have to begin to live like a caveman because you will already be living like a caveman. Unless of course the end-of-the-world scenario includes a mutant virus, nuclear winter, alien invasion or the nanotechnology-gone-awry black goop and then your only real hope is to be in a type two end-of-the-world scenario instead of a type one scenario.

Type two in the end-of-the-world scenarios is a lot more promising because no matter how horrible the end of the world is, you are a member of a special group of believers who will be transported to a new world in a new dimension, in heaven or in a fully restored earth or possibly some other planet. This is no ordinary end of the world, this is the apocalypse, and for those in the know it is the ticket to a better life and all that is necessary is to believe the correct beliefs and for everyone else to be mercilessly wiped out by your god because they got it wrong. Pretty simple and compelling case for joining a cultic sect just in case. The quandary, of course, is which one? It wouldn't be too good to be believing in Thetans with the volcano worlds of Xenu and the Galactic Confederacy with the religion of Scientology if those Jehovah's Witnesses knocking on your door with *The Watchtower* got it right and the Tetragrammaton is going to keep you and the other 143,999 believers safe. Thetan. Tetra. Thetan. Tetra. How is a person to decide on a cosmic insurance policy against the unpleasantries of the end times?

As a cosmic voyager through all times, dimensions and universes, I hope to help you understand these possible end-of-the-world scenarios, including making the right belief choices to keep yourself covered, and how to make a fabulous fortune on the misfortune of those caught up in the end times. To learn more, you must stop trying to read this book for free if you are in a bookstore and take it immediately to the checkout counter where you will pay for it before proceeding further. YOU MUST GO TO THE CHECKOUT NOW. If you are not in a bookstore but are reading a friend's copy, then you must give that friend an amount equal to the cover price of this book to continue. DO IT NOW. If you are reading this online, then you must voluntarily pay a similar amount to the cover price using the convenient PayPal button located near this text. NOW. When you are done reading this book you must pass it on to another person. They will pay you when they get to this page of this book, don't worry. If you either do not pay for this book or do not pass it on to the next person, your wife, husband, girlfriend or boyfriend will dump you, you will become depressed by your failed romantic life and forget to water your houseplants which will wither and die and you will lose your job because of your changed demeanor, at the very same time as the insurance runs out from the job you lost you will contract a serious illness which involves uncontrollable flatulence, and even worse bad things will happen that I don't have the heart to describe in these pages, but it is unimaginably nasty and involves lime Jell-O, if you get the drift. DO NOT TEMPT YOUR FATE by not buying this book and then passing it on. This is not a chain book, this is really true.

Now, that you have bought this book, and before you pass it on, send $1 to each of the names below, cross off the bottom name and add your name and address to the bottom of the list. Sit back and wait for the money to roll in.

You know just six months ago, my car had been repossessed, I had an eviction notice on my door and not a penny in my pocket (in other words, things were pretty normal). Now based on the money-making plan I have outlined for you, I plan to be buying a brand-new luxury car and an ocean-view condo in which to enjoy my instant-wealth retirement. I feel so fortunate, I want to share it with you, my loyal reader who has paid for this book by now or who will be cursed to the end of time and beyond if you have not.

If you believe that someday you deserve that lucky break that you have waited for all your life, simply follow the easy instructions below. Your dreams will come true, unless your dreams are like my dreams which are mostly nightmares and then you will be blessed that your dreams will not come true, but that is even better.

Do not break this chain, even though this is not a chain letter and is not illegal, so don't break the chain. Remember the lime Jell-O.

This is a literary work and I am providing a product or service to you, so this is not a chain letter or chain book and the U S Post Office Inspector, the Internal Revenue Service, and the Central Intelligence Agency have no reason to investigate and if they do, I want the investigator to know that I have been the victim of identity theft and it is a different Nosirrah who wrote this book, I am not the same one that you got for that Amy Bruce chain letter, you know the one that started,"Hi, my name is Amy Bruce. I am 7 years old, and I have severe lung cancer from second hand smoke. I also have a large tumor in my brain, from repeated beatings. The doctors say I will die soon if this isn't fixed, and my family can't pay the bills. The Make A Wish Foundation has agreed to donate 7 cents for every name on this list. For those of you who send this along, I thank you so much, but for those who don't send it, what goes around comes around. Have a Heart, please send this."

That was a different Nosirrah that looked just like me, but it wasn't me, although I thought the combination of the heart-wrenching plea and the implicit dark threat of something "coming around" was pure genius on the part of the Nosirrah who wasn't me. And by the way, for the record, Nosirrah is not. I am not Nosirrah, but neither is he. More on this later or you might want to pick up a copy of my tour-de-force novella *God Is an Atheist* for more on the not that isn't Nosirrah.

So, don't worry about legal issues, just follow the instructions by sending $5 to the first 4 names and adding your name to the bottom after crossing out the top name before passing this book along.

- Nosirrah c/o General Delivery, Nothing, AZ
- N. Nosirrah c/o Sentient Publications, P O Box 6071, Boulder, CO
- Nosirrah c/o General Delivery, Oak Knoll Sanatorium, Sonoma County Hospital, Sonoma, CA
- N. Nosirrah c/o General Delivery, Albrightsville, PA

Perhaps this is a good time to segue, which is a fine word derived from the Italian *seguire,* to follow, originally from Latin *sequitur,* which also means to follow, so it shouldn't surprise you that the word *segue* means to move to the next thing that follows immediately, like a section of music segueing into what is next in the piece. The word is used in writing as a way of describing a smooth transition that keeps the reader from noticing that there is a shift in subject due to the logical connection to the prior subject. Truly skillful writers can take their readers from the first word to the very last without the reader even noticing that they are reading a book, much less a book that has no depth of subject matter or purpose of plot. But, I am not such a writer, I am sorry to tell you, and you will notice transitions, you will notice gaping holes in the logic, spaces so large that you will fall into them even while grabbing for the sides of the text to hold onto to stop your fall into the abyss of your own nothingness. But, you cannot hold onto this text, to the patched together net of meaning that you have assigned to these words so that you will not fall further into your own non-existence. You are at the end of your world, the end times are here, and you can trot out all the importance you can muster but there is no segue from nothing, nothing follows The End.

Except, perhaps grace, for it is grace that has you reading Nosirrah, rather than a skilled writer who can move you along with artful segues, oblivious to your dilemma and impending doom. By grace, you have come to this book, and Nosirrah has written it, and Nosirrah is a student of the arcane, the unwanted, the discarded. Look deeper at *segue*, at the Italian *seguitor* from whence it comes, and to the Latin *sequi*, at the whole notion that something follows. Do you see your freedom? Look harder! Nothing follows anything. The musical analysts got it wrong, the smooth writers got it wrong, the Italians, the Latins, everybody got it wrong. Nothing follows because nothing comes before or after, nothing causes what occurs, logic doesn't connect the dots of our life, there isn't a connection, there is just dots. Do you see your freedom? Just look at the dot, not the imagined connection to the last dot or the next one, this is your doomsday where all your meaning melts into vacuity and this is your freedom where all your anxiety enfolds into equanimity. No connections, nothing to connect to, just one thing, nothing before or after. Your logical fallacy is that because you have a thought that suggests your continuity, you are continuous. But, dearly beloved, your thought is just a blip, and the world it suggests is just a blip with it, and you and your logical fallacy are just a blip, and all the blips together simply are not.

It isn't sequitur, it is non-sequitur that runs the universe. Abrupt, illogical shifts; paradoxical occurrences; electrifying transitions—welcome to the non-sequitur universe, an acausal world which is about to end—again. And again. And so forth. And if Nosirrah is the master of anything, he is the master of non-sequitur, therefore he mocks the pretend Masters, the charlatans, those who make the connections of cause and effect, he laughs at them and calls them the silly names they deserve. Nosirrah is a Master baiter, but only when he is frustrated and lonely. But that was really a non-sequitur, a bad pun and possibly a little too revealing even for a semi-autobiographical, tell-all, self-help, think-and-grow-rich, survivalist manual cum novella such as this.

But before I change the subject, you might find it interesting that I, Nosirrah, was, in a prior life in the early 16th century, John of Leiden, a twenty-something millennialist apocalyptic prophet of the end times in Munster, the German city which then held some ten thousand believers. In true Nosirrahian style I declared myself King of Zion and Messiah, and began running the region as King of Z, instituting polygamy and banning private ownership (and all books except *The Bible* of course). I was eventually overrun by the mainstream Christian forces in the area, tortured as the mainstream Christians of the day loved to do, and along with my two main followers hung from the main Cathedral in iron cages where we were left to rot. The cages are still there, by the way, now a tourist attraction much like the cathedral itself, with torture being relinquished by the church and turned over to the able pliers and waterboards of patriots who are willing to use it to protect us, or alternatively use it on us, depending on whether we answer the fruits and vegetables question truthfully on the customs forms when we come back to the USA from overseas.

As John of Leiden, I was a millennialist. My basic idea was that things were going to go bad, really bad, pretty much it was the end, with the battle with Satan and all of that, then there would be a thousand years of heaven on earth. Now, as John, I did believe that I was the Messiah, but there was a slight error in that idea. In fact, I was Nosirrah living in a medieval guy's life and that temporal stretch did make me seem pretty ethereal and I could whip up the crowds. There is something really rock and roll about the end of the world and the good times on the other side. In the fifteen hundreds you could wear leotards, and prance back and forth, calling out to the crowd, "Let me hear you say, 'End Times!'"

"End Times!!"

"I can't hear you!"

"END TIMES!"

"Fire and Pain."

"FIRE AND PAIN!"

The bladderpipes and crumhorns were wailing, and I would do my trademark harpsichord riffs. I did a little number on stage, a quick split, or sometimes if I was feeling the juice, a back flip, and then worked the front of the stage where the groupies hung out screaming their medieval heads off and grabbing for a piece of me. I wasn't really God, but I was a Rock and Revival God and sometimes it seemed that was even better, until they locked me up in the iron cage to rot, and then it was pretty evident what the difference was. As I said, there was a small error on my part, which I have taken up with God directly as I have recounted in my semi-autobiographical novella *God Is an Atheist*. It did take me many lifetimes to get it all straight about me and God, but I try to look at it on the bright side and say to myself, "Today is the first day of the rest of your past." But that all depends on your temporal perspective, as we do tend to look at time as if it has a particular direction and as if we exist right at the place where the past breaks one way, the future the other. So you couldn't say,"Today is the second day of the rest of your past,"because that would place you someplace other than where you are in the timeline, which is where we presume we are since we presume time is linear and moves from past to future, rather than simultaneous, or as I like to think of it, all at once. You could say,"Today is the second day of the week" but you could say that only on Tuesdays, unless you are a Seventh Day Adventist and then you could say it only on Mondays, which in any case would leave you without cheery but meaningless aphorisms most of the time, but I think you get my point, and if you didn't it is entirely possible there wasn't one.

Although, possibly my point was that we have a profound question in our lives about the presence of a vast and incomprehensible universal energy we like to make comprehensible and small enough to fit into our tiny neo-simian brains by using the word *God*, as if that word meant something. Well, God does mean something, according to Merriam-Webster (the God of Dictionaries) it means the supreme or ultimate reality, the Being perfect in power, wisdom, and goodness who is worshipped as creator and ruler of the universe or the incorporeal divine Principle ruling over all as eternal Spirit or infinite Mind or a being believed to have more than natural powers requiring human worship and controlling a particular aspect of reality or possibly just a powerful ruler. But what does that mean? Take out your *Bible, Koran, Torah, Upanishads, Dhammapada, Book of Mormon,* or *Dianetics* (that's the Scientology text, if you don't have a copy of *Dianetics* you can use the source material as originally published in the 1950 edition of *Amazing Science Fiction*). Now all seven billion of us have out our sacred books, start reading it out loud, no shouting please, let's be respectful of our brothers and sisters of different creeds, we are not trying to convert anyone here, this is just a novella, no one has to get hurt unless I say so, of course, but I am having a pretty good day so things in my book should stay peaceful. So read from your texts of world wisdom and faith. Ready, get set, gophers. Tricked you. Try again. Ready, set, go!

OK, OK, OK! Whoa, that doesn't sound like it is helping us understand God, it sounds more or less like gibberish. For those who are only reading this book and not hearing these voices in their head, here is what it sounds like:

> *Buddhists chanting: All that we are is the result of what we have thought: it is founded on our thoughts, it is made up of our thoughts. If a man speaks or acts*

with an evil thought, pain follows him, as the wheel follows the foot of the ox that draws the carriage.

Christians reciting: In the beginning God created the heaven and the earth. And the earth was without form, and void; and darkness was upon the face of the deep. And the Spirit of God moved upon the face of the waters. And God said, Let there be light: and there was light. And God saw the light, that it was good: and God divided the light from the darkness.

Jews reading:

1 ץרֶאָהָ תאֵוְ םיִמַשָּׁהַ תא םיהִלֹאֱ ארָבָּ תישִׁארֵבְּ:

2 תפֶחֶרַמְ םיהִלֹאֱ חַוּרוְ םוֹהתְ ינֵפְּ־לעַ ךְשֶׁחֹוְ והֹבֹוָ והֹתֹ התָיְהָ ץרֶאָהָוְ
םיִמָּהַ ינֵפְּ־לעַ:

3 רוֹא־יהִיְוַ רוֹא יהִיְ םיהִלֹאֱ רמֶאיֹּוַ:

4 ןיבֵוּ רוֹאהָ ןיבֵּ םיהִלֹאֱ לדֵּבְיַּוַ בוֹט־יכִּ רוֹאהָ־תאֶ םיהִלֹאֱ ארְיַּוַ
ךְשֶׁחֹהַ:

EDITOR'S NOTE: A SECTION OF A SACRED TEXT OF A PARTICULAR MAJOR WORLD RELIGION WAS ORIGINALLY PLACED HERE BY THE AUTHOR, WHICH WOULD PERHAPS EVOKE WORLD RIOTS OR WORSE, HOWEVER IT HAS BEEN REMOVED SO AS NOT TO OFFEND THE RATHER ROUGH FUNDAMENTALISTS OF THIS PARTICULAR RELIGION. WE WON'T TELL YOU WHICH RELIGION IT IS THAT WE DON'T WANT TO OFFEND BECAUSE THAT MIGHT BE OFFENSIVE TO

THAT RELIGION. WE HOPE THAT THIS EDITOR'S NOTE WAS NOT OFFENSIVE, AND FOR THAT MATTER WE HOPE THAT OUR WISH TO NOT OFFEND IS NOT OFFENSIVE, AND IF IT WAS OFFENSIVE, WE APOLOGIZE FOR THAT AND ANYTHING ELSE WE MIGHT BE FORGETTING, NOW, IN THE FUTURE AND PAST OR ANY OTHER ANY OTHER NON-TEMPORAL REALITIES ON BEHALF OF THE PUBLISHER AND ITS HEIRS OR ASSIGNS IN PERPETUITY, SO HELP US GOD (YOUR GOD, NOT OURS, HOPE THAT WASN'T OFFENSIVE). IF INDEED WE HAVE MANAGED TO OFFEND, WE WILL NOT ATTEMPT TO PROTECT OR PLACE IN HIDING THE AUTHOR OF THIS BOOK, BUT WILL HAPPILY SACRIFICE THE AUTHOR, AND TWO INTERNS OF YOUR CHOICE, JUST CONTACT ME AND I WILL TURN OVER HOME ADDRESSES, PHOTOS AND WHATEVER ELSE IS NEEDED TO GET THESE VERMIN.

The Hindus intone: In the beginning there arose the Golden Child; as soon as born, he alone was the lord of all that is. He established the earth and this heaven:—Who is the God to whom we shall offer sacrifice?

He who gives breath, he who gives strength, whose command all the bright gods revere, whose shadow is immortality, whose shadow is death:—Who is the God to whom we shall offer sacrifice?

The Mormons are knocking on doors, saying: . . . remember the things that ye have observed concerning this people; and when ye are of that age go to the land Antum, unto a hill which shall be called Shim; and there have I deposited unto the Lord all the sacred engravings concerning this people…

…And now I bid unto all, farewell. I soon go to rest in the paradise of God, until my spirit and body shall again reunite, and I am brought forth triumphant through the air, to meet you before the pleasing bar of the great Jehovah, the Eternal Judge of both quick and dead. Amen.

EDITOR'S NOTE: WE ARE TRULY SORRY TO INTERRUPT THIS TEXT ONCE MORE, BUT AGAIN THE AUTHOR HAS INSERTED SACRED TEXT WHICH WE FIND INAPPROPRIATE, IN THIS CASE FROM DIANETICS AND THE TEACHINGS OF SCIENTOLOGY. WE ARE JUST AS TERRIFIED OF THE SCIENTOLOGISTS AS WE ARE OF THE FUNDAMENTALISTS OF THE CERTAIN PREVIOUSLY UNMENTIONED MAJOR RELIGION, BY THE WAY, BUT IN THIS CASE WE ARE REMOVING THE TEXT OFFERED BECAUSE WE DO NOT THINK THAT ANY INFORMED READER WOULD BELIEVE THAT THE REMOVED TEXT COULD POSSIBLY BE PART OF A RELIGION UNLESS IT WAS A RELIGION COMPRISED OF SCIENCE FICTION BUFFS OR FIVE-YEAR-OLDS OR THE VERY UNLIKELY POSSIBILITY OF A RELIGION COMPRISED OF FIVE-YEAR-OLDS WHO ARE SCIENCE FICTION BUFFS. THE TEXT THAT HAS BEEN REMOVED SUGGESTED THAT SCIENTOLOGY TEACHES THERE WAS A DICTATOR OF THE GALAC-

TIC CONFEDERACY NAMED XENU WHO, ROUGHLY 75 MILLION YEARS AGO, BROUGHT BILLIONS OF HIS SPACE PEOPLE TO PLANET EARTH IN A 1950s AIRPLANE-LIKE SPACESHIP, PLACING THESE SPACE PEOPLE AROUND VOLCANOES ON EARTH BEFORE KILLING THEM WITH HYDROGEN BOMBS AND THAT THE GHOSTLY REMAINS OF THESE NUKED SPACE BEINGS ATTACH TO US EVEN NOW CREATING SPIRITUAL DESTRUCTION. WE ARE NOT MORONS AND YOU ARE NOT A MORON, AND NOBODY COULD POSSIBLY BELIEVE THERE IS A RELIGION IN THE TWENTY-FIRST CENTURY THAT INCLUDES THIS KIND OF MATERIAL AND WE DON'T KNOW WHAT THE AUTHOR WAS THINKING INCLUDING THIS KIND OF SHAM MATERIAL IN HIS OTHERWISE ADROIT TREATISE ON THE-END-OF-THE-WORLD-AS-A-METAPHORIC-END-OF-THE-SELF. I DON'T KNOW ANY SCIENTOLOGISTS, BUT MY BEST FRIEND'S COUSIN MARRIED ONE, AND THEY SEEM TO BE PRETTY NORMAL AND THEY NEVER SAID ANYTHING ABOUT DEAD SPACE BEINGS SCATTERED AROUND VOLCANOES, ALTHOUGH COME TO THINK OF IT, WHY IS THERE A VOLCANO ON THE COVER OF THAT *DIANETICS* BOOK? AND WASN'T THE FOUNDER OF SCIENTOLOGY A SCIENCE FICTION WRITER? WELL, NEVER MIND, WE TOOK OUT THIS SECTION AND THAT IS THAT. AS BEFORE, WE WILL GLADLY TURN THE AUTHOR OVER TO A SCIENTOLOGY EXTRACTION TEAM IF THAT WILL BUY US PEACE AND SAFETY.

Dear Reader, this is Lydia Smyth, the editor of this magnificent work, speaking to you in a stage whisper, so that the Scientologists will not hear, so that other readers will not hear, writing to you now as I must completely outside the form, the text, and movement of this dynamic novella and tell you that I believe that Scientology might find experimenting on Nosirrah with their dreadful electrical gizmos is actually a contribution to the human race, if indeed Scientology, as it is said to do, can reveal the complete recording of Nosirrah's past lives to him. Imagine a Nosirrah, the man that I love, but can no longer bear to see, who is entirely clear. Imagine him fully bathed, possibly shaved and the periodontal disease in remission. Envision his eyes bright, shining, with both orbs going in the same direction. Now take this restored man with the benefit of a free personality audit and some not so free followup to get him across the bridge of total freedom. Can you see the Man that Nosirrah would be if his mind wasn't a stream of consciousness mixed in with the flowing discharge from a cosmic sewage treatment plant, if his deep insight into the nature of human consciousness wasn't fixated on seducing women, taunting psychiatrists into their own psychosis and pursuing his infantile question of whether or not he is actually a dog? In other words, if this man could be Scientologically cleared into a Man, then I could once again hold him in my loving arms, binding him gently but firmly with those bumpy knots that dig in if you struggle, and punishing him for his philandering, his wanton womanizing over many lifetimes, with others who could not possibly love him with the ferocity, the perverse creativity that I have in which we pushed not just the boundaries of decency, but the edges of reality itself. I am becoming overheated. Dear reader, I had to tell this to someone, I have no one after all, just endless days and nights working with these idiot-savant writings of Nosirrah, but how I long for the Man behind the man behind these writings. Now you know, but only you, and you also know that as I tempt the Scientologists to take him, I know that they can only liberate him and themselves in the process. When they are done with him, he will also be done with them, and they will no more be Scientologists in that moment than he will be Nosirrah. I must cool down with a cold shower and some Barry Manilow, god, how he dislikes Manilow, but that is another matter and I will return you to the main text with my thanks for your listening and for your discretion.

Second note from Lydia Smyth: I am so embarrassed. I just got a screaming message on my voice mail, which I almost erased thinking it was a crank caller doing a rather bad imitation of Tom Cruise when I realized it was Tom Cruise doing a rather bad job of acting as if it was not Tom Cruise calling. I never did think Tom could act that well, but he was kind of cute in that fighter jet pilot movie and that other one where he danced around in his underwear with his cute little buns that you could just imagine cradling in… but I am straying from my story, and in any event, Tom still can't act but now his nose has gotten really big and his eyes are all buggy. But, whether this was a screaming Tom Cruise pretending to be someone else, or someone else pretending to be Tom Cruise is not the point (although I did hear a weak voice in the back ground that did sound a lot like Katie Holmes say, "Help, get me out of here, I am being held against my will by science fiction buffs…"). The point is that the caller informed me in no uncertain terms and at the top of their theatrically trained voice that Scientology does believe in Xenu and the spacepeople and the volcanoes and all of that, it is just that they don't want anyone to know that until they have gotten you all signed up, credit card info collected, last four of your social, and at least through the first couple of courses to clear you. While I still find this hard to believe, I did google Xenu, and Tom Cruise or his sound-alike may be correct. If so, I retract everything I said, especially about having to be a moron to believe this sort of thing, and of course if the Scientologists believe this then I want to apologize for any errors I have made in a very clear statement, which might be something like, "Please don't hurt me, I, Lydia Smyth am just the figment of the imagination of the mad genius Nosirrah and he makes me do and say things that I cannot control, and he himself is a figment of his own imagination, and so too, dearest, kindest Scientologists and Tom Cruise and/or Tom Cruise impersonator, you, your religion and all your beliefs are a product of your imagination, so that you can see that you, I and Nosirrah are one, and this one is not." Xenu, on the other hand, I am not sure about. I now return you to the text of the novella.

And that does bring me back to the point which was long ago lost in my meandering narrative, which was the question of the unknown, that which we are not sure about or can never know. There is a vast center of knowledge imbedded in my mind that I believe in, my ideas, concepts and learned responses, the aggregation of sensations, feelings, emotions and thoughts that this wondrous biomachine called Nosirrah has collected, protected and espoused through his long years. I have read so much, I have learned so much, I have experienced so much, that I know that I know. Unfortunately, regardless of how much I collect in the knowing department, however vast my collection becomes, there is one little tiny piece of knowledge that eats away at my certainty. That knowledge is that I know only what I know, and I can never know what I do not know, and further, and this is the most unfortunate further that you can come across in life, what I do not know is so colossal that it makes my vast knowledge become relatively miniscule and absurdly meaningless. In other words what I know is a cosmic joke, a constructed sense of security, a childish denial of my actual place in the universe, which is a speck of a speck without any bearings at all.

I can know all about the proper way to fillet a fish, how to solve a quadratic equation and the major river systems of Asia, which as a matter of fact I do. But, when I allow myself to consider the full extent of the universe, I don't really know anything of significance. I will put it more succinctly, more precisely, more knowledgeably: I do not know anything.

I can discuss the nature of satori, the meaning of the Eucharist and nature of the imminent God versus the transcendental God, but when I look from what I know directly at what I do not know, I see God laughing at my hubris. Well, more accurately, God is laughing. I, in my hubris, think he is laughing at my hubris. As speck of a speck, I am not, and God is laughing at the notion that I am. When I met God, as I recounted in my must-read, chart-busting novella for those who have run out of time, *God Is an Atheist,* the ultimate joke was that the God I met was not, therefore did not believe in himself and certainly did not believe in me. If you have not purchased this important book, please do so immediately as one thing I do know with absolute certainty exists in the universe is the royalty check, and quite honestly I am a bit late on my rent.

Although I have told the tale of meeting with God, I have never really talked about my encounter with the Devil. Now you will find this ridiculous if you do not believe in the Devil, and you will find this blasphemous if you do, but I did meet the Devil and in fact I was introduced by God.

"Nosirrah, this is the Devil, Devil, this is Nosirrah. I think you will find a lot in common." God did what was like a cocktail party introduction, where the host tries to connect you to someone else to take some of the social tension off and then disappears into the kitchen. I don't know if God went to the kitchen, but he disappeared.

"How do you do, Devil? What do I call you, Mr. Devil or Devil or what?"

"You can call me The Devil, but that is a little formal, you can call me Lucy D, forget Lucifer, I always hated that name, can you imagine going through school and having the teacher checking attendance:"Lucifer Devil, are you present."You know how cruel kids can be, well, I was asthmatic on top of everything else, probably from all the sulfur fumes, so I was just picked on from first grade on.'Lucy Fur, what kind of name is that! That's a girl's name. Deviled Eggs, Deviled Eggs, here comes Lucy the girl.' It took me years of running and hiding before I could face the taunts of those kids. I realized that there was a feminine side to me, and maybe it wasn't so bad to be a girl. I did secretly like to cross-dress, so I just came out of the closet and started to strut my stuff in middle school. Lucifer Devil became Lucy D and I was hot, no pun intended, but not just hot, but smoking hot, red hot, hellishly hot. I had the boys and the girls drooling in carnal temptation. I was in four-inch heels, fishnets, hotpants and the skimpiest of tops. Even the teachers were getting the hots for me, so I was thrown out of school by ninth grade. But, it didn't matter, I had found myself."

What is interesting about the Devil is that she is very open and available to talk about her feelings, the pressures of being a celebrity evil deity and transvestite and the very real, down-to-earth, actually down-to-earth-and-below girl behind that pitchfork. She seems like she has it all, celebrity, power and a large fan base of those who believe in evil, damnation and hell. But, when I sat down for a chat with her while she sipped on a Diet Coke, there was an unexpected and vulnerable side to the Devil that came out.

"The thing is, it isn't easy being Me," she confided. "Sure, people run in terror when they see me, and that's great and all, but they are also trying to destroy me. It is the little things, you know, like all the crucifixes held up as I go by and the holy water thrown at me. It gets old."

Of course, I had to ask her what drives her, what motivates her to get up every day and face the world as the worst nightmare and most evil force in human consciousness.

"That's just it," she said leaning forward for emphasis, "I am really nothing at all. It is my fans who create me. Their fear and hatred sustain me. Without them I am nothing."

But, I wanted to know how this intriguing revelation could be true. After all, the Devil threatened all of humankind with eternity in Hell. That wasn't nothing, there was a pit of torment, a lake of fire, an endless chasm of despair.

"Au contraire, mon ami," Lucy D laughed, her nostrils flaring in an endearing yet bone-chilling way. "Where I reside is a place of absolute vast nothingness, an empty space that has no beginning or end. It is you who brings the Hell with you. It is your mind, your fear, your separation that encapsulates you in endless torment."

"What is funny," she continued, "is that Heaven is the same vastness. Everyone arrives on the same elevator and when the door opens what you see is what you are. Even I, the Devil, am just an expression of your fear. There is nothing that I am without what you are hiding from and what you will not look at.

Look at yourself and you will see what I am, and if you look deeply enough you will also see what I am not. I am not evil, I am the illusion created by ignorance and denial."

Although I had come to believe I was a *People* magazine reporter getting some good celebrity gossip, I realized that I was really going to have trouble with the interview. Lucy D's eyes had turned blood red, her horns almost seemed to be sharpening themselves, her serpent tail flicking from side to side. If this was my fear, then I must be very afraid, because even though I knew this was only my mind, my mind was freaking out. Lucy D had grown red and scaly, her face contorted, her hands claw-like, reaching to remove my heart, still beating, from my chest.

Lucy D's eyes had turned blood red

"Nosirrah, get a hold of yourself,"I screamed to myself.

Lucy D screamed back,"I do have a hold of myself" and laughed a hideous but strangely alluring coquettish cackle as she held my still beating heart up in the air. I do have a hold of myself? Were Lucy D and Nosirrah the same? I am a non-dualist, but this is going too far, I thought non-duality meant I was one with good things, happy things, spiritual things. I didn't want to be one with nasty, horrible things, and certainly not Satan in the form of a transvestite or Lucy D in the form of Satan or whatever it was I was encountering. If I had to be one with everything, this was really going too far and duality began to look pretty appealing. I began to make a list of all the spiritual seminars and retreats I had attended, considering how to get a refund on my investment in enlightenment. Oneness is not everything it is advertised as.

"Nosirrah, this is just your mind. There is no Devil, no Lucy D, no evil, there is only what you fear and what you create from that fear. Let it go and there is nothing."

"OK," said Lucy D, and she let go of my heart, which hit the ground with a thud, which if you have ever had your beating heart ripped out of your chest, held high and then dropped to the floor, you know that really hurts, although if I am honest with myself it was kind of a turn-on as well, but that is probably just me.

What was I missing? I knew that evil was in my mind, I knew my mind was deranged, well, really all minds are deranged, occupied as they are with thinking, therefore I knew that the experience I was having was entirely imaginary. The problem was that the experience was so vivid, so full of details, that it was entirely convincing, I couldn't escape the details, I couldn't escape the Devil. So, it was true after all, the Devil *is* in the details.

We are so absorbed by our senses and the narrative that weaves them together as experience that we take the experience to be what is happening. What is happening is not our story of what is happening, not our paltry attempt to describe the endless stream of sensory input. Our description is a lie, it is a lie of convenience because if we don't tell ourselves we know what is going on then we will know that we don't know what is going on and that would be much worse. We cannot admit to ourselves that our brain is trying desperately to find coherence in an endless stream of nerve input that tells us little or nothing about the totality of what is outside the prison of skull. The brain is a bubble boy who can never actually touch, smell, see or feel. It can never breathe, or sigh, or yell in ecstasy. It can only process the endless data stream in total silence. The brain cannot know anything first hand, there is no direct experience other than that silence.

Do you think that you see with your eyes? Tell me then, why is it that the vast majority of fibers coming to your visual cortex don't come from your retina, but from brain areas related to memory? You don't see the world, you construct it and included in that construction is the idea that you are seeing. You are guessing, not receiving, bumbling through life building models of what is going on based on faulty memory and incomplete sensations. No wonder it all feels like a dream.

You might think I have concluded that all I can know is that I cannot know, but no, my friend, my dear reader, you who have invested your hard earned coin in this tome of truth—and let's face it, sitting on a median strip facing traffic with a cardboard sign, "Need New Book by Nosirrah, Any $ will Help?" is not as easy as it may look—, that we cannot know is, after all, a conclusion, not a question, and Nosirrah is wedded to the eternal question, not a question of the mind and its intellect, but questioning the mind itself and all of its spawn.

In my time in Ancient Greece, I could not say, "All I can know is that I cannot know" as a conclusion and while I took this up in my discussions with Socrates and later Carneades, who defended this humble notion, I was of the Pyrrhoic school, which found hidden delusion in the statement. More to the point of how limited our brains are in the face of the vast universe is the realization that that we cannot know anything, and that we cannot even know that we cannot know anything.

The nature of a dunce is that he is not even aware that he is a dunce. I was not attracted just to the essence of knowing nothing at all, but that from that knowing nothing we can see the source of human pain. Pain is when we know something. By qualifying anything in knowing it, we transform it from what it is in actuality, to what we know, which is imaginary. What we know is now something, not nothing. That something carries with it the weight of the past, of the conditioning, the memory burden that is anxiety, fear and separation. We pay the price in fear, but we buy with that our sense of substantiation. I am fear, but at least I am.

I would rather have a cross-dressing Devil smashing my heart to the ground than face the unfortunate truth that I can't accurately know even the nature of my own breath in, let alone the breath out and all the attendant sensations and phenomena. I don't like not knowing, although anyone who knows what they are talking about knows they are confused. I want to know that I know or at least know that I don't know but I cannot live in the state of total energy that is not knowing at all. As they say, better the Devil that you know than the Devil you don't know, or pretty much anything else that you don't know, or something like that. There is another one of those Devil in the details things because not only can I not remember the saying about the Devil you know but I can't even remember where I was going with this sentence other than there are a lot of Devil phrases. Speaking of the Devil, it is a Devil of a job to avoid Devilish phrases that ultimately put a writer such as me between the Devil and the Deep Blue Sea, which in this case is putting me between Satan, a she-Devil slamming my heart to the ground and my editor Lydia who will not like the meandering prose (and then, believe me, then there is the Devil to pay) and she really won't like the repeated use of the word Devil even if it is cleverly weaving in numerous Devil may care phrases. It is Lydia who has slammed my heart to the ground with her denial of our carnal love. She edits even this text so as to deny that she has caused me more torment then any Devil could, changing a phrase here, a word there, so that you the reader will come to believe that I, Nosirrah, am the one who is deranged, that my meeting with the Devil is just literary license, not a metaphoric accounting of my tumultuous affair with Lydia. Perhaps I am recounting an actual and profound meeting with Satan, I do, after all, like to keep my readers guessing. Nevertheless, Lydia, you are the Devil in my life, you have broken my heart, still beating. You are the Deep Blue Sea and I must choose between the Devil of my mind and the Deep Blue Sea of my past with you. I must choose between the six headed monster Scylla and the whirlpool of Charybdis.

Here I must call out to myself, "Nosirrah, snap out of it. You don't have to do this to yourself. Forget the Devil and Lydia. Steer the ship between the Devil and the Deep Blue Sea, watch out for the monster, watch out for the churning whirlpool! Are you not Odysseus?"

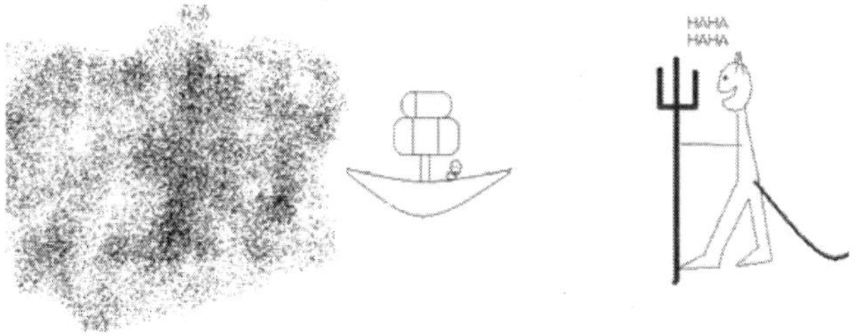

Steer the ship between the Devil and the Deep Blue Sea

Yes, though it is difficult for a person of even above average intelligence to comprehend, Nosirrah is not bound by time or space. He lives in all beings, in all times, for when cosmic consciousness pours forth through the temple that is his pock-marked, rickets-ridden body, Nosirrah can appear as anyone in any time. For most, they watch the hour glass slowly pass its grains of sand to the chamber below. For a jnani such as Nosirrah, he watches this same hour glass, but he is doing so from the shirshasana position, that is the yogic headstand, inverting himself and time in a mystical union with all that is, all that was and all that will ever be.

In short, Nosirrah is Odysseus. I am Odysseus, a trickster, a cunning survivor of oracles and lover of women.

When they wanted me to go to war, I feigned madness to get out of the army's draft, plowing my fields with salt in crazy patterns so they wouldn't conscript me. I was a sane person in a mad activity.

But, that damn Palamedes put my son in front of the plow and I demonstrated my sanity by stopping the plow. Like it or not I was off to the Trojan War to retrieve Helen. I had become a sane person in a mad activity.

Then in the search for unity I became a mad person in a mad activity and killed Palamedes in revenge.

Ten long years I traveled from adventure to adventure, searching for home, finding my way through from the travails of total madness—or was it total clarity? I could no longer tell. Maybe you can tell me, are you a sane person living a life of madness? You probably think that sometimes, but let me tell you the truth, your life is perfectly sane, it is you that is crazy, just like Palamedes. He couldn't be sure that I was faking my madness, yet he put the boy in front of my plow, and I, of course, even I couldn't be sure if I was faking my madness, I had gone so far into character. I found out only when I stopped, the plow blade just gently touching my boy's little forehead.

Sanity does not lie in the idea of it, that sanity is merely a social construction in which you may assemble yourself in or out of madness. These constructions are not stable and we cannot know the energy that lies beneath what we know of the mind. We are comfortable in the mind structures, but there is the energy of life which knows no morals or mercy, has no limitations because it has no center and no boundary, and this energy will tell us whether we are sane or insane, not from our constructs but in the crackling instant, the timeless moment when we either stop the plow or we do not.

Odysseus's journey is the voyage to the edge of the universe, to the pits of hell and the confluence of the rivers Styx and Acheron, to the abyss, to the place between the Devil and the Deep Blue Sea where life itself manifests without cause, without time and without you, or me. He is a hero not because he survived to tell the tale, but because Odysseus, because I, Nosirrah who is Odysseus, did not exist other than as myth and so could not survive in actuality, and yet I still tell the tale. The Hero is the one who is not, who realizes that he is not and does not resist this fact. The Hero is the expression of the collective forces of all the universe, not an individual narrative, but a mythic narrative, a story so vast it can explain itself only with gods pulling the strings of human marionettes. The Hero has no free will, only the appearance of choice, the gods laughing at the hubris of such a puny speck aspiring to do the right thing. The Hero knows he is a speck, knows his choice is not a choice, knows the right thing cannot be known and knows the gods are laughing, but because he is the mythic Hero, he knows one thing more, and that is, while the gods may be laughing, toying with man, the gods themselves are not, they are just a evanescent manifestation of the timeless universe, a creation of the men whose strings they pull, an aspect of the story that humankind tells itself, not beyond the story, but in the story. The great Hero knows that there are no gods and hence no Heros, that the marionette strings that pulls his hands and feet and make his mouth speak words are not guided by the hand of a manipulative God, but are guided by nothing at all, occurring just like all things out of nothing at all and fading, like all things, into nothing at all.

Odysseus understood and when the Cyclops asked his name he told him,"Nobody."When Odysseus attacked the Cyclops, the call for help was a strange but true exclamation,"Nobody is attacking me!"Of course, Odysseus, nobody, escaped. Nothing happened to nobody. That is the deeper meaning of myth, there is nobody for anything to happen to, and so there is nothing that ever happens, all that there is then is narrative and that is very clearly just a story. So it is with our lives, just a story, nothing ever happens.

I am a great Hero, I am a god, I am Odysseus, I am Nosirrah and I am all and I am none. Call me crazy, but when I dance the dance of the puppet I am dancing not from the guidance of an unseen energy but as that energy. Shiva dances as the energy, dispelling illusion, the Dance of Bliss, Anandatandava,

The Dance of Bliss

as the endless movement of creation and destruction. Odysseus, Shiva, Nosirrah are one and are not, and the not is dancing.

This is why the end of the world is such a fascinating topic. Creation we get: we do things, we make things, we do the pokey-pokey and babies appear. But destruction we know only so far, we tear things down, we fight and we kill and we do all of that very well, but we cannot know about our own non-existence.

Even the guy on the street corner who looks like he has stepped out of a *New Yorker* cartoon doesn't get that. He had "The End is Near" sign and handed me the pamphlet with the description of how it would happen. I had to set him straight because there are a lot of people fighting over how the world is going to end and there is no consensus at the moment. I shared with him the various theories on how the world would end, and after considering the length and breadth of the possibilities, he became quite upset because, I suppose, he liked the way the world was going to end according to his version of things, but didn't so much enjoy other people's end of the world endings. You would think that it wouldn't matter much how the world ends, just if it ends, but I guess that is the difference between "The End is Near" where you have some time to disagree and "The End" where there just isn't any time, so there isn't anyone to disagree.

Just so you know, the leading theories on how the world will end are:

- Global Warming, Al Gore was right and we didn't listen;
- Global Cooling, Al Gore was wrong and we didn't listen;

- Rogue Nation or Terrorist nuclear explosions, Nuclear Winter and we all glow together when we go;
- Giant Meteors colliding with earth and we join the dinosaurs in the past tense except there is no one in the present tense to read about us;
- SuperVolcano eruption, lava and ash pretty much ruin the environment;
- Mass loss of reproductive capacity from chemical pollution, good news is school taxes go down, bad news, the race dies out;
- Invasion by Space Aliens and humans exterminated just because the aliens can, since this is pretty much what happens when an advanced civilization moves in on a more primitive one (by the way, in case you are not following this, *we* are the primitive ones);
- Universe is actually massive computer program and program is finished (or someone trips over the cord);
- Baked by ultraviolet radiation due to loss of ozone layer and sunscreen won't help;
- Mutating Viruses turning us into flesh-eating zombies and the world into a gore fest;
- Mutating Viruses just simply killing us without bothering to turn us into anything;
- Satan arriving with a very negative attitude;
- Nano-technology goes awry with out-of-control, microscopic, self-replicating robots consuming all resources, turning the world into gray sludge;

Flesh-eating zombies

- Cloud computers take over using relentless machines with Austrian accents to hunt humans;
- God getting mad and raining down fire, brimstone, serpents or any number of other nasty things;
- Biological Warfare where someone sprays the enemy without checking the wind direction;
- Malthusian catastrophe or some form of famine where eventually even the Mormons run out of food;
- Nearby star going HyperNova and frying the earth to a crisp;
- Nearby star is the Sun, runs out of hydrogen, starts to burn helium, consequently expanding to 250 times its current size, swallowing up Mercury and Venus, turn-

ing Earth into a baked dessert before it is pulled into the Sun and vaporized, the only good news being that the best guess is all of this will happen between 1 and 8 billion years from now, although it is good to prepare for these things ahead of time;

- The Large Hadron Collider, the giant particle accelerator in Switzerland, actually works and scientists produce a tiny black hole which then swallows up the entire world;
- Mass suffocation due to anoxic event, the oceans lose their oxygen and that is that for the air supply;
- The Rapture with the righteous true believers rising to heaven and the rest unpleasantly surprised that their theologically adventuresome beliefs and atheistic theories were just plain wrong as they are plunged in the fiery furnace of Hell;
- Dysgenics creating utterly stupid human race which self-extinguishes (note this might already have happened, can someone check on that?);
- Gamma ray burst from outerspace, black hole incident, vacuum phase transition or other cosmic incident where we are irradiated, disassembled, or otherwise made very dead;
- The Mayan calendar runs out on the Winter Solstice, Dec 21, 2012 and time ends, but nobody is too clear what this means or even if it is true, so there is a little concern that when time ends everything ends;

- Perhaps worst of all possible doomsday scenarios is the deep, conscious inspection of reality itself and the ensuing insight that thought and reality are one, that thought is insubstantial and that reality therefore isn't and we are not and poof, ipso facto ergo incognito caveat emptor abracadabra that is The End.

Since it is clear that there is no real security, that the end can come in an instant, then we can focus on what is important, which is to make money.

Let's just use a simple system like the ads running in the newspaper, "Make Money Working from Home, send $25 dollars" and when you send in your money they send back a sheet of paper that says,

1) Run an ad in the newspaper that says "Make Money Working from Home, Send $25"
2) Wait for the checks to come in
3) Send a copy of this letter to each person who sends a check.

I improved on that system by running an ad that just said, "Send $25" and that saved me the trouble of sending back anything at all.

I heard about another system where you raffle off a Jaguar sports car, collecting $100,000 from people by selling a thousand tickets for $100 each. The winner gets a Matchbook replica Jaguar that is worth maybe $5. Now you are probably asking yourself, doesn't the winner usually get pretty angry about the misrepresentation when he gets the toy car? Of course he does, so you refund him his $100.

I have never tried that one, but it seems like it would work pretty well. I am always looking for minimalism, so I refined the idea. I sold tickets to an enlightenment seminar to a thousand people for $100 each, I told them I would give them the experience of nothing and that is what they got, absolutely nothing, and they thanked me on the way out. Now *that* is a system.

The end of the world presents some unique wealth building opportunities. Let's say it is going to end on the Winter Solstice in 2012 because the Mayan calendar runs out on that date. As I have written in my magnum opus novella *God Is an Atheist,* imagine the opportunities in real estate, used automobiles, jewelry, small appliances and furniture, not to mention stocks and bonds, as the believers unload their earthly possessions in anticipation of the end of the world in 2012. After midnight on December 21, 2012, you start selling it all back to them with a markup plus storage and handling fees. That is how to profit from the prophets in the coming end of the world. Storage is the issue if you are trying to hold onto the possessions of six and half billion people for six to twelve months, and I have written before that you could just throw a tarp over it all and hope it doesn't rain. But after some more consideration, I think it might work to use all the domed sports stadiums as giant storage units, because if time is going to end will anyone care about sports? Maybe Red Sox fans, but they don't have a domed stadium anyway.

Here is the other detail I have worked out, because many people wrote somewhat unpleasant letters after the publication of my tour de force tome *God Is an Atheist,* many suggesting that I was an imbecile, which I keep meaning to look up, it sounds like it might be French for genius. Readers thought it would be impossible to buy the possessions of the world's population, who has that kind of money, but let me tell you the secret that I know you are reading this book to find out. The secret is to use Other People's Money to buy their possessions from them. Using OPM, you can buy it all, everything on the planet just before the asteroids hit or whatever is the finale du jour. You offer a promissory note for the purchase price, and since it is the end times, that should be about one cent on the dollar, secure it by the pile of stuff you have already accumulated in the nearby stadium and make it due and payable on… and this is where we must pause to appreciate the rare intelligence shining through Nosirrah…you make the promissory note due and payable *the day after Doomsday!* If they were right, the world ends and the debt disappears along with the rest of the world into a black hole or a heavenly afterworld. But, if they are wrong, the world doesn't end, you sell their underwear, toaster and living room furniture back to them for a nice markup of let's say 100 times what you paid for it just days before, pay the note off and keep the difference. Now aren't you glad you bought this book!

Maybe you don't appreciate the idea of great wealth and lest I confuse you, I must tell you that I don't care a wit about wealth myself, I just have assumed that you are the one concerned about riches beyond your dreams or why else would you buy a book about profiting from the unspeakable horrors of the end of the world? You bought the book, I am just a simple writer and visionary. You were intrigued by the idea of making money from the ultimate misery of humankind. I will now tell you something which will help you understand just how crass your interest is in profiting from the end of the world.

You may already know that the title of every major novel such as this one is tested with focus groups, random polling and data mining. I had originally titled this book, *You Are Greedy and Narcissistic, but Don't Worry About It Because It Is All Illusion Anyway,* however extensive research indicated that not a single person had even a remote interest in buying the book, in fact, people would not take a copy for free, often throwing the sample in the face of the unfortunate marketing staffer. The marketing people floated a new title: *The Secret Power of Love, Sex, Money and Weight Loss Guaranteed with the Ancient Tibetan Yoga Zen Way of Crystals.* This title was wildly popular with the focus groups, snap polls indicated an amazing 93 percent would buy it immediately even if they were down to their last $24.95 and data indicated that it would sell twelve million copies in the first twenty-four hours besting those Potter books (which I never did understand anyway, I grew up living under the stairs and I never saw any wizards unless you count my hallucinations, and, boy, were there some spooks flying around in those visions!). The head executive at the publishing house was practically hyperventilating when he called to give me the news about the new title, saying that we would all be rich and he could finally dump his wife and take up with the new intern who was embarrassingly too young for him and wasn't even remotely aware that he was fantasizing about reading manuscripts together with her on some remote Caribbean island. In his mind he had practically spent the fortune that he was going to make on this new title. He was a man in near ecstasy.

But, he didn't realize that he was dealing with a man such as Nosirrah, one who is not moved by either wealth or poverty, but whose one dedication to life is discovering the absolute truth at the core of existence, which presumably involved getting to know that intern a little better.

Nosirrah stands in the truth and when I heard the new sure-to-be-successful title, *The Secret Power of Love, Sex, Money and Weight Loss Guaranteed with the Ancient Tibetan Yoga Zen Way of Crystals* I knew I could never agree to it, I could not put my name on such a book, for while I considered myself the world's foremost expert on Love, Sex, Money and Tibetan, Yoga, Zen and Crystals, the harsh truth was that I could not represent that I knew anything at all about weight loss and this would be evident to anyone who had the misfortune of finding themselves in bed with me without having removed all light bulbs from the room, being blindfolded, being legally blind or for the best possible outcome, all three. In short, while my animal magnetism is without peer, my body does demonstrate that total disregard for caloric intake is not a pretty sight.

I explained to the apoplectic publisher that his plans with the intern were entirely unnecessary and even perhaps spiritually damaging to all concerned. He should consider that the wife and intern were one, and that while the wife was a faded fifty-something- year-old shrewish complainer who spent her days switching channels between Home Shopping Network and *Maury!* and the intern was an idealistic, intellectually stimulating, athletic, mid-twenties hottie, only his mind made the distinction between the two of them. Freedom from distinctions is absolute freedom. Further, I suggested to him that he would be free of his desire for wealth not just when he embraced poverty as coequal, but when he ceased to reference either quality—wealth or poverty—as a description of life. I took his piercing screaming to be a sign that he was deeply moved by my counsel and so I told him the Hassidic tale of two men who wanted to understand how to accept the good and bad that God delivers to us as equal blessings. To understand this question the men were sent by their teacher to visit with a mystical Rabbi who would answer their question. They found the Rabbi living in a shack in near starvation with rags for clothing obviously living a very difficult life. The Rabbi was surprised to hear his visitors were sent by the teacher with their question. "Why did he send you here? I have never experienced anything bad in my life!"

I have never experienced anything bad in my life!

I think that this helped the publisher executive because while he became more or less catatonic and from what I heard never returned to his office, he did apparently join his wife on the couch watching TV at least until the eviction took place, but no doubt he was unconcerned when he, his wife, the couch and the television were all placed on the sidewalk by the sheriff's men.

Meanwhile, the intern was promoted due to the executive's sudden retirement and since she was in charge I had to have multiple late night meetings with her to refine the title. I find it helps my creativity to lie in bed when working on my prose, even more so if there is an idealistic, intellectually stimulating, athletic, mid-twenties hottie collaborating and in this case she was able to help me with some of the Pilates positions I had been having trouble with, being quite limber as she was, which I believe would have ultimately resulted in an even better title for the book although in the end I don't remember actually discussing the title during our time together. I am certain given enough creative time, we could have come to the perfect title, but my editor and jealous former lover, Lydia, stepped in to stop our communion and had the intern's two-week career as a publisher terminated. I was forced to accept Lydia's own title, which is the one on the cover of this book.

Marketing did not like Lydia's title, and polling showed only three people would buy the book, you, dear reader, being one of them. But Lydia was not to be denied and she got her way as she always does.

I tried to protect my literary work and I protested but Lydia would have none of it. She believes that she is protecting me and like a mother grizzly bear she is fierce in her defense, unyielding in her actions, as well as smelling like a mix of decaying salmon and fermented berries, which I think more than explains my obsessive attraction to her. She believes that I am one who has no guile, who cannot fend for myself. "Nosirrah," she said, "you are a man who knows nothing" and I could not disagree, for if there is one thing I know, it is nothing and that nothing is one thing, and there is no second to that one.

It seemed to me that this was almost a cinematic moment, and I wandered off into a reverie as I often do, imagining a rewrite of the classic Hitchcock film with Doris Day singing in the title song of *The Man Who Knew Too Much Nothing* and I was spinning off into a dream of that movie. I was dreamer and the dreamed, having merged with Doris Day who had merged with my new best girlfriend, Trixie, who always wants money and seems to have a lot of other boyfriends, and my own mother, Alice B. Toklas, merged with Scarlett Johansson as the Earth Goddess working on the endless construction of reality itself, all set to music that sounds a lot like "Que Sera, Sera":

When I was just a little boy,
I asked my mother, "Alice B?
Am I enlightened?
Am I crazy?"
Here's what she said to me:

"Nosirrah, sirrah,
Whatever you see, will be;
You construct reality.
Nosirrah, no 'me'!
......If you see, you're free."

When I grew up and fell in love,
I asked my sweetheart, "Do I owe you?
I see you an hour,
Day after day?"
Here's what my sweetheart said:

"Nosirrah, you slob,
This isn't love, you see,
My love's sold for a fee.
Que sera, sera,
Your spear's the size of a flea."

Now if I had children of my own,
They'd ask me, "Nos, What's with your brain?
Why so frenetic,
Is it genetic?
Will it happen to me?"

Oh, tra la, la la,
Life's singular, not two;
Held in sync with cosmic glue.

Plus a paper clip or two,
........That's Reality.

"Nosirrah, sirrah,
Whatever you see, will be;
You construct reality.
Cause there is no 'me'!
......If you see, you're free."

You may be wondering what any of this has to do with the end of the world, and admittedly I have wandered far from the topic, except in truth we are never far from the end and therefore never far from the topic of the end. You may also wonder how this work could be considered a work of fiction, filled as it is with such ontological profundity and vacant as it is of any obvious plot line. I will address these issues now and shall do it with the fewest possible words so that I can get back to the meandering prose that will be recognized as genius once the professors of the humanities, the theologians and philosophers catch up.

Here is the plot and here is how it relates to the topic of the end. *You* are the plot line, baffled though you are, you weave a tale you call reality. You are non-existent save your narrative that you are. When you see that you are only a story, then you have come to the end of it. Life continues, just without your story. So, the end is the beginning. Life without your story has no plot and no topic, it just has pure vita.

Now let's get back to plot and the topic.

While we may love our story and the thinking that tells us it is true, thinking is becoming more or less obsolete. Thinking is a model of the world which we apply as we collect data. We used to collect data and test it on a model. If the data fit the model, then this was declared to be truth. This worked really well when the data was simple, for example the sun rising and the sun setting, obviously the Sun revolved around the Earth and we could collect that data everyday, agree to the truth. Then the Polish guy named Copernicus started collecting more data and it looked like the Earth was going around the Sun, and he was smart enough to die just after publishing his work, so the Church only got to burn his followers at the stake but even the Church got over it eventually and agreed that it was a heliocentric world we occupied. This is the legacy of science: data collection and new models to test. What a great tradition! But, now data collection capacity is going through the roof and basically you can collect unimaginably massive data points, so much data and so much complexity that you can't fit it into any model, rather, the data *is* the model. If you step on a million grains of sand at the beach with your foot, you get the imprint of your foot, an aggregate of a million events as one. In other words, we can't look for patterns in infinite data, the infinite data extrudes the patterns.

If I collect every bit of information on you, from your genetic makeup, to your credit card purchases, from your respiration rate to your family photo album, and I aggregate that data, I do not need a model of you to suggest what you would like to eat, what clothing you would like to purchase, what book you would like to read, I don't need a model of you because I have *you*. You are the manifestation of that information, the universe forming the imprint of you out of a million million million grains of itself.

The Large Hadron Collider will produce 10 petabytes of data a second, much more than any system can handle and only by reducing the amount of information to that amount in a year can scientists even look for evidence of the strange superparticles they are seeking. What lurks in the data they cannot look at is the actual universe, just as what surrounds our own thoughts is the vast space of totality that is beyond thought, and beyond consciousness itself.

Faced with petabytes of information, the need for models disappears. But the thinking mind is constructed of a continuous series of models, and so the thinking mind must transform to the streaming mind or be left with the stale assumptions that its limited capacity has proven to itself. The mind after all is designed not for enlightenment but for superstition, ever expanding superstition, but superstition nevertheless. Can the streaming mind keep up with the endless data flow of the universe? Not so long as there is any model at all, not so long as thought is considered to be a representation of what is. But when the streaming mind is the endless data flow, without separation, well then we may begin to see the human potential unleashed, or perhaps we will see madness, but doesn't it depend on who is defining such things?

Nosirrah has thrown himself into the stream, his thoughts are just the belches of one who has eaten too much cabbage and onions with his cantaloupe, which by the way is considered a delicacy in the small, minaret-free village of Pfungen, Switzerland where I was snowed in for an entire month in a barn with just the cows, a dairy maid named Heidi and the entire fall crop of melons, onions and cabbage. Heidi was very impressed that I was a descendent of both Arnold Winkelried and William Tell, which in some sense I am as I have merged with all beings, and such merger with the heroes of Helvetia allowed me to demonstrate the sureness of my arrow throughout our time together exploring the Tantric dimensions of cross-cultural contact. Unfortunately Heidi and I were interrupted by the end of winter celebration of Sechseläuten by the village peasants, which as you probably know from your study of Swiss culture is the festival where the Bogey Man is burned, or as the quaint Swiss call him, the Böögg. Doubly unfortunately for me, it turned out that the lovely Heidi was the Mayor's daughter and the Constable's betrothed, so they decided I was the Bogey Man for the year and dragged me to Zurich, yodeling all the way, to set me on fire in the city square. You may recall that in the custom of these peaceful people, the Böögg's head is rigged with fireworks and the speed with which the head explodes predicts a rainy and cool or dry and hot summer. You may wonder how I survived to write this account, and it is that while the Swiss are very good at interest rates and chocolate, they are a little susceptible to the illusions of the material world especially when they have been drinking damassine, the prune wine they love so much in the Alps. Yes, you guessed it, I substituted a cantaloupe on a pole for my explosives-rigged head, slipped out of my burning clothes and joined the crowd as they cheered the detonation of the melon they took to be Nosirrah's head. It was going to be a hot dry summer, but it was time for me to move on.

And, so I shall move on, I shall step into the streaming mind and see where it is flowing.

Is the streaming mind madness or the vanguard of a new consciousness, not even Nosirrah knows, but will you dare to find out, to step into that stream and be swept away? If you judge Nosirrah, in what superstitious certainty do you stand to decide upon his state of being?

That superstitious mind is itself just a speck of aggregated data in an infinite cloud of data of all people and all things, each a clump of tendencies and probabilities. This is the universe manifesting reality, a reality far too vast for the speck to contain. Worse, the speck (that is you), like the footprint on the beach, has the appearance of solidity but is in fact empty. The footprint tells us something about the universe, but there is nothing there, the footprint is empty space defining form, extruding information while at the same time itself nothing at all.

You are the footprint and so am I, empty. Yet, that emptiness defines form that tells us a great deal. You are empty, yet everything you are not, like a lost wax casting, predicts with mechanical certainty what you have been, what you are and what you will be.

You doubt this but I can predict with confidence what you will do next. Even though you and I have never met, I do know you. You are attracted to obscure novellas and particularly to their rather modest price. You are a hopeful person, willing as you are to read through pages of turgid prose in order, you hope, to get to something which will suggest that you did not entirely waste that rather modest amount paid for this book. You have become disconnected from a cherished relative, friend, work associate, pet or possibly someone who is listed in your hometown (or some other) phone book either by circumstance, disagreement or death, one who left something unsaid but who actually cares for you more than you realize. By the way, does the number 5 mean anything to you, perhaps part of your home address, your credit card number or your phone number?

All right, think of any number from one to a thousand, and please do not tell me what that number is. Now double that number and add four to it. I will tell you with certainty that it is an even number and not an odd one. You may try to explain away my prescience by saying I had an equal chance of guessing odd or even, but I will allow you to try this again with any other number you may pick and don't even add the four this time. I will tell you that your number is even, and I will not only be correct, but I published this prediction even before you had acquired a copy of the book! I predict that you are now amazed.

What you will do next? I can tell you that you will read this sentence. Do you now see what I mean? Of course you are confused, wondering what it is I am trying to say, thinking about whether the bookseller will take the book back even though it has been thrown against the wall a few times. I knew that! I think you will have to admit that I have proven my point.

If enough data is sampled, what is manifest is known, then it would seem that you are just an expression of that which is known, a collection of information swimming in a sea of information, a proverbial salt doll swallowed by the ocean, but that is not the end of it, for you and your merged ocean and your salty spiritual metaphors are surrounded by vast and endless lands of exformation, empty spaces in which there is no data, no information, there is nothing to sample, yet the shores of this nothing give the very shape to the sea, and the sea gives form to you. You are not then, in your essence, what is known as it would appear, but rather what is not known. You are not.

You cannot believe that you are not, for you have your firm beliefs, your certain knowledge, your history and your aspirations for what is to be. After all, don't you read these very words with your eyes, consider their meaning with your mind, all the while aware of the slight movement of breath, the stomach too full or too empty, the heart craving for solace and love? Your certainty comes with your unflagging belief in your awareness, that by being aware therefore you know. But can you reflect for just a moment on the silliness of such a proposition? What you are aware of describes one thing by excluding everything else, and it is the everything else that makes up practically the entire universe, while that of which you are aware is a meaningless footnote to the universal everything. You build your imagined empire from these less than minor details and declare yourself at its imaginary center. So you are right after all, you do exist, just that it is an imaginary you in an imaginary world as an imaginary center. Enjoy the virtual world, you dreamer, you.

I have declared myself to be done with the virtual world, limited as it is to the mirror-gazing-at-mirror of my own illusion. I have declared that I am not and that my allegiance is no longer to what I am aware of but is now and henceforth to that which I am not aware.

Nosirrah is not a man or a mystic, he does not even write these words, nor has he the amazing past of a tantric savant recounted in the pages of his other works, for while I have had each of these experiences of decadent love or sublime transcendence (and in the case of the dominatrix sacred dance teacher in Barcelona as recounted in *Chronic Eros*, decadent transcendence, not to mention the debauched Flamenco duet we performed in the middle of Placa de Cataluyna to the amusement of the passersby, you would never believe castanets could be used like that and as gendarmes explained is not legal anywhere in Europe let alone in a public square,"!Mi amor sus castenets me ha tocado profundamente, ouch!")—but to the point, despite the experience, the experiencer is not, I am not, Nosirrah is not.

And, if you are reading a book that was never written by a writer that never was about experiences that never had an experiencer, then can you be so sure that the reader is? If you are not, then your world is not, and it is Doomsday everyday, Armageddon at breakfast, End Times at lunch and Final Judgment at dinner with no let up from non-existence.

You may think that is a bad deal and resist with everything you've got, insisting that you are an existent, sentient being with a history and a future, but your insistence, loud as it may be, falls upon the deaf ears of the same nothing from whence it came. You are exhausting yourself with your attempts to generate something out of nothing, a being out of nonbeing, and when you fall silent, having worn yourself out, the silence that you have become will meet the silence that you have always been, joined as it is with the silence that is the all and everything, and you will be exactly what you are, which is not.

Your last line of defense is either ignorance or apathy. What is the difference between the two? I don't know and I don't care. Now that is an old joke, but not the oldest joke, which in English is a thousand years old, and here is how the oldest of old jokes goes: "What hangs at a man's thigh and wants to poke the hole that it's often poked before? Answer: A key."I can keep going here, but I think you have come to prefer non-existence to another old joke. Pain, it would appear, can be the gateway to truth.

Haven't you been looking to liberate yourself from the bounds of your self? If you seek to enlighten yourself and end up losing yourself in the midst of your search, have you failed or succeeded? If you are non-existent and the non-existent world that you inhabit ends, has anything happened? If the end of the self is the beginning, then what is all the talk about a middle way?

As to spiritual enlightenment, if you had never heard of the term *enlightened*, could you ever be enlightened? Once you heard the term *enlightened*, could you ever be enlightened?

For that matter, if human ignorance can be transcended with enlightenment, then if I transcend enlightenment does that mean I can go back to being ignorant? In the beginning, neurotically chopping wood, carrying water, then enlightenment. After enlightenment, neurotically chopping wood, carrying water. And, this has really been bugging me, why do ignorant people seem to be having a lot more fun?

Most fundamentally, if the world came to an end and nobody realized it, would trees still fall in the forest?

Am I making any sense here? I hope not, because if you are making sense of what I am writing then you are missing the point. And, really, how many angels could dance on that point, or maybe angels dance on the head not the point, but that is my point, it is not the head that needs to make sense, nor the dollars and cents, nor the scents of a woman (though for Nosirrah that is the point, his point and the woman that is, and that is pretty much a double entendre, pardon my French). Life is not logical; it just is without explanation, without rationalization and without anything prior.

I want to take a moment to attend to more mundane matters for those of you who purchased this book in the hopes that it would give you clear instructions on surviving the end of the world. Survivalist organizations publish many lists of what you need to take with you when you flee the end of the world, in order to insure that there continue to be survivalist organizations, and I have done extensive research into the many lists. These lists involve so much stuff that you might as well stay home because all that you need is right there. But, for those who refuse to stay home and will be clogging the freeways while the aliens zap them with energy beams, and are expecting concrete and specific survival information from this book, then my research suggests that you collect the following: gallons of water, trail mix, first aid kits, flashlights, credit cards, birth certificates, safety pins, space blanket, plastic trash bag, parachute cord, plastic water bag, iodine-based water tablets, large cotton bandana or triangular bandage, 9-hour candle, waterproof matches, disposable lighter ,magnesium fire starter, magnifying lens, whistle on lanyard, stainless steel double-surface signal mirror, flashlight with fresh batteries, surveyor's tape, Swiss army knife, knife sharpener, hemostats, sharpened piece of hacksaw blade, extra-heavy-duty sewing needle, heavy-duty rubber bands, compass, snare wire, canned food, maps, radio, extra eyeglasses, Pepto Bismol, plus the Mormons suggest you bring along Scriptures, Genealogy

Records and Patriarchal Blessings. I can't really vouch for the Mormon scriptures, but alternatively I think it is always good to have a copy of *The Necronomicon* along just in case the end of the world should involve Yog-Sothoth or Cthulhu. I believe that, in addition, you should include at least one copy of each of my books, which encode the most profound wisdom of the human race to date and are excellent for fire starting as well, and perhaps some duct tape and paperclips because they seem to come in handy. And potato chips for comfort food. And, maybe an AK-47 assault rifle or semi-automatic handgun and lots of ammo, just because you are a sportsman and might want to do some target shooting.

The Federal Emergency Management Agency suggests you pack everything into an easy to carry container for quick evacuation. I prefer to pack everything in to an easy to drive Hummer. And if you have time, fill up the tank before the lines get too long at the gas station as they tend to do when the world is about to end. The only other thing I would suggest is if you have a little time between the end of the world warning and the actual end of the world, take extensive martial arts training, short the stock market and do your laundry. Lastly, should it be the situation that you are left with a large alien robot named Gort from a planet 250 million miles away which is going to destroy Earth, remember to say, "Klaatu barada Nikto" which should stop the destruction, presuming the aliens haven't changed their password, which they might do after they read this, so never mind.

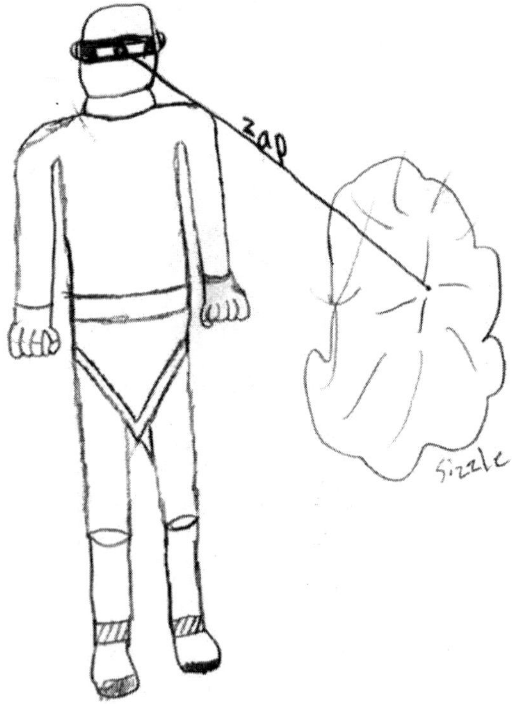

A large alien robot named Gort

I believe the above should cover everything for the reader who wants clear survival instructions, and there will therefore be no need to complain to the publisher or the beleaguered bookseller, and certainly no point in complaining to online booksellers like Amazon since they will likely, in their cheery but soullessly automated fashion decline your request and suggest that you contact them again if you have any further questions, and again, in fact, it doesn't really matter how many times you contact them because there is nobody there but an automated response from a giant cloud of computers pretending to be Sarah or Thomas. You could try "Klaatu barada Nikto".

Now that we have dispatched the survivalists who are busy packing their gear, we can get back to the real point. We are not afraid that the world will end, just that *our* world will end. The world will do just fine without us, all of us. Whatever horrible things we do to each other or to the earth, really, the natural world doesn't care. We could dump plutonium mixed with ground up plastic mixed with automobile emission gases and mercury-laced coal burning residue all over each other and all over the earth from the Arctic to the Antarctic, from the redwood forest to the Gulf Stream waters. We would die, but life would adapt, perhaps over millions of years, but no one would be around to count the years, so life would just adapt in a moment and spawn new life in new forms. Come to think of it, we *are* covering the earth with mercury-laced plutonium, plastic, poison gases and a lot more. We have melting ice caps, huge garbage plumes in the oceans, pesticides in our food, mercury in our waters and air, Fox News on our televisions, and I don't mean to disparage garbage, mercury and pesticides by grouping them with Fox News. We care about the issues of our existence; we try to clean up, we argue over how to have our lifestyle and our survival. Life doesn't seem to care. It is unconcerned with our survival, it is too busy mutating, adapting, dying and creating what is new. It is not just that it is too busy, it is that even if life was on vacation at an eco-resort relaxing with a tall, cool glass of locally grown, hand squeezed, organic lemonade, Life doesn't see the human being the way the human being sees the human being. In fact, Life doesn't see the human being, it just sees itself, it sees Life, interconnected, indivisible without liberty and justice for all.

We are narcissists. We think this is about us. We believe that we have been given dominion over all that flies and walks and swims. We believe that our 401K with Morgan Stanley will supplement Social Security and give us a decent retirement. We believe that non-existence is an abstract concept invented by French existentialists but the Invisible Hand of the Market Economy is real.

Life doesn't read French. Life is the ultimate narcissist; it has nothing outside of itself to refer to and nothing within itself to know. Life does not think it is about life, it doesn't think at all, it just is. Nothing has dominion over life, not even death, certainly not humans. Life doesn't believe in Morgan Stanley, rather index funds is where it would place its fate, the natural movement of all things without the hubris of human guidance, minimal capital gains and a very low fee structure. Life is what occurs in the face of non-existence, it is the something that emerges from the nothing, including the nothing, subsuming what is not into itself.

You see, my friends, the world doesn't end, just your world ends. Are we concerned with the dying frogs, the disappearing butterflies, the endangered snail darter, or are we concerned with the fact that we humans should be on the endangered species list—we are killing ourselves, our environment and our future. The poor animals on the endangered species list are just spotted owls in the coal mine, harbingers of what is to become for us.

The hell with the human race, in truth, I am concerned that *I* am endangered, I wonder if this is my last breath, if I have cancerous tumors, if my heart is about to stop pumping. What about me? I would trade the humans and the freaking endangered species and the non-endangered species, along with my Reggie Jackson baseball card from 1977 for a guarantee on my own life.

I would trade it all to survive, even if it meant being in the *Twilight Zone* episode where I am the last guy on earth, but I would rewrite it so that there was an Eve to my Adam, and a Sue Ellen, Roxanne, Shawna and Ashley, and I am suggesting a five to one ratio not just due to my polyamorous leanings and uninhibited libido, but I would dedicate myself to population regeneration as my life purpose and believe that I am really the best man for the job having trained for it all of my adult life. Yes, I see that this boorish drive to womanize is just a denial of my death, but it is working so far.

I don't want to die, I don't want to suffer, I don't want to become impotent, wrinkly or bald (or I would like to reverse those conditions as the case may be) and I would like to have a young woman on each arm, and unlimited credit on an American Express Black card and you can have the rest of the humans, the animals, most of the plants and all of those who cannot be categorized as animal, mineral or plant (like for example take Donald Trump… please).

I just want to survive, me, me, me, me. That is why I recycle and vote for the Democrats. Republicans scare me, don't they all look like velociraptors, all beady eyed and ready to strike, especially the Republican women (and, yes, I include Ann Coulter) and all the Republican men are way kinky in the bedroom, but then they are always confessing their sins, and going to church for absolution and starting all over again with the interns or the office assistant, but maybe that is part of the kink for them, a kind of erotic religious fervor.

I do good things and vote for good people not because I am good, but because I want to survive. I do the right things for the wrong reasons which I have decided is better than doing the wrong things for the right reason and likely to be superior to doing things randomly for no reason at all, which usually lands me in an involuntary psych hold, and if you have ever been in a straightjacket and had to itch your private parts, you know that it is not the place you want to be unless you happen to be Harry Houdini and then you would most certainly be dead since 1926, which would negate the whole point of trying to survive by doing good things, because you can't survive if you are already dead, unless it turns out that there is an afterlife and then survival really depends on having the right belief and going to the right church, temple or mosque while you were alive which is why I would like to state here for the record that I believe in all religions, jointly and severally, as being the one true religion and I have visited religious places of worship frequently enough in my estimation to qualify under almost any afterlife scenario with the only real problem being if either there is no afterlife, or if no one on earth has it right, like for example if there is nothing after you die then there is not a whole lot you can do about it except possibly scream at the top of your lungs as you approach death,"I don't want to die!!!"which I have tried when I think the bus driver is not going to stop at a red light, which is quite often actually, and I think I am going to die as a result of the impending crash so I start screaming and this has led to me being asked to no longer ride on public transit, but I do feel better than if I wasn't screaming, because what if the bus driver runs the red light and we do all die in a fiery crash and I don't make a sound, or maybe, like my aunt says, it is better to die peacefully in your sleep like my uncle, then to die screaming like the other three he was driving home that night, but maybe they were trying to fend off death, so think about it next time you are riding a bus or here is another possibility which I haven't really worked out, maybe you just die and the afterlife has nothing at all to do with any religion or spiritual belief system, like let's say that you get a heavenly afterlife if you always passed gas when you needed to rather than holding it until a more opportune moment or you get a good afterlife if you were always polite to telemarketers instead of asking them for their home phone numbers so you can call them back when they are likely to be sitting down to dinner, so you could end up dying and finding out that you are going to burn in hell or plunge into nonexistence just because all the religious guys got it totally wrong and then you would be totally screwed. (I note that my editor says I need more punctuation so the reader does not become confused, so please distribute the following as needed in the prior section: … .,,,,?????;;;; and !!!! Let me know if you need more.)

You cannot be too careful. I am the only one I know who wears sunblock in the tanning salon. That would be SPF 100 to be exact. And I never actually turn on the tanning lamps, I just like lying in the coffin-like apparatus knowing that I am not inducing skin cancer. That womb-like feeling of safety for an hour a week at the salon results in a radiant look when I take to the streets, well perhaps not radiant, rather a reflective look since light bounces off white on white quite nicely, the combination of pasty skin with the pallor of a corpse and the aforementioned sunblock slathered on top. You may think me a fool but I will bet that you did not realize that a dark tanning bed blocks ultraviolet radiation very nicely, reducing the possibility of skin cancers to practically nil. I tried living in a tanning bed for an extended period of time, figuring that I would therefore never have the chance of skin cancer, but instead I developed bed sores, claustrophobia and severe bruises. The latter condition came about only while I was being removed by the store manager upon his discovery of my personal dwelling set up in the seldom used Bed 14.

My point is, though, that you cannot be too careful. Recently I became quite involved with perfecting my diet, eating only the best low-calorie organic raw vegan foods in the most limited quantities, presuming that by perfecting my diet I would escape all disease, stop aging, live forever, become fashionably emaciated and be quite enlightened. I don't smoke, drink, do drugs. I have a long-term yoga practice including three hours a day of meditation. I earn what I need and give what I don't to indigent orphans with terminal illnesses. My resulting life is so pure that I am in ecstasy around the clock. You will have to try it. It is also the most boring monotone existence you could imagine, so to jazz things up a little, I do have one little vice. I am a chronic liar. I lie about not smoking, drinking and drugs, my pure diet, my yoga and meditation and that I actually have an income to give away. I have a horrible diet, seldom leave my basement room, can't stop pacing long enough to do yoga or meditation and haven't been employed since the tics started.

I do have one good aspect of my life, though, which is I have a rich imagination and no discernment between what is real and what is imaginary. I often confuse what I would like to be with what I am. Or to paraphrase the great Taoist philosopher Chuang Tzu, am I a phobic dreaming I am perfect or am I perfect and dreaming I am phobic, or possibly a butterfly having a really horrible nightmare that I am Nosirrah? Or am I Chuang Tzu not dreaming at all since in reality Chuang Tzu was a third century invention of Kuo Hsiang?

A butterfly having a really horrible nightmare that I am Nosirrah

I am not telling you anything you don't already know, but Kuo Hsiang not only created Chuang Tzu, one of the most famous Taoist philosophers of all times, but then became famous himself for writing commentary on his creation's writings. And to take things one step further, Kuo Hsiang's commentary was really a rewrite of the material of another Taoist named Hsiang. Kuo Hsiang's name was originally Kuo but he became known as Kuo Hsiang despite the fact that neither Kuo Hsiang nor Chuang Tzu existed. This would be like saying you are reading a book by Nosirrah and Nosirrah does not exist. And that is exactly what you are doing, and indeed, Nosirrah does not exist, he is simply the creation of my own mind, and I should know since I am Nosirrah.

Now, may I repeat the obvious question—are you so certain that you exist? Please look into it, as your concerns about the end of the world may be considerably diminished if you discover that there is no one to be concerned, no one to die and no world to end. With this realization you could declare yourself a renowned commentator on this very book and its important message for humankind. There is nothing to stop you. If you are not, then you can be anything at all and no one can prove you are not, because no one can prove that you are.

For Chuang Tzu, also known as Kuo Hsiang, also known as Kuo, the world has no before or after, it is generated spontaneously and without causation. Nothing is at the heart of it all. Creation moves of its own generation and in that occurrence sets the conditions of all that is. To put it another way: you are not, except as a spontaneous arising, and then, I am sorry to inform you, you are totally responsible for the whole universe because what you are is what it is. It is not a good deal, but it is the deal you've got. Things are the way they are, you didn't make them that way, but you still have to deal with it through the action that is non-action. Non-action is not just sitting around, it is the action that doesn't come from an actor, doesn't make distinctions and doesn't look for particular results.

Perhaps the one issue I have with the Taoist fundamentalists is when they say, paradoxically, that those that know don't say and those that say, don't know, which is more or less a self-negating statement. I assume that they know this for a fact, but by saying it, that would mean they don't know. The problem is that if the Taoists didn't say it then nobody would know it, so they can't just shut up because then nobody would know that shutting up was really profound. People might just think the Taoists were simply quiet or shy or really stupid, so in Nosirrah's proposed Reformed Taoism, you have to say that you are silent because you are beyond words so that people know. Then those people will talk to each other to discuss what it means and seem very unenlightened since they are not silent and you can hang out in the silence and be pretty much in control of the situation.

You may wonder where the writer of this tome stands in the who-speaks-and-who-knows-what game. Is Nosirrah enlightened? I will say this, that I, Nosirrah, never claimed to be a good Taoist, never claimed to know, and while Nosirrah certainly speaks, he does it in the shortest possible books and in a non-linear fashion that some would say borders on gibberish. But, it is enlightened gibberish without a doubt.

Further, while many have sought my counsel and teachings, I am just a freakish fool, an oddiot, and yes that is a word created by my second son, B. Nosirrah, in his attempt to understand who I am by creating a convenient category, a sub-species, a cross between an idiot and an oddity. The second son, along with the first, have attempted to piece together their childhood, raised as they were by a strange mystic who cannot be bound by expectations of anyone, especially those too little to change each other's diapers. I have described the tumultuous circumstances of these Nosirrah offspring in a chapter in my quasi-allegorical autobiography, child rearing manual and travelogue cum novella, *Practical Obsession,* and shall not go into any more details here other than to say that A. Nosirrah and B. Nosirrah may say what they like about their childhood with me now that they are men, but everything I knew about parenting was learned by my deep study of World Wrestling Federation matches and as I always told them, tap out if you are ready to submit, or as I used to sing them to sleep,"tap out before you black out, tap out or it's a knock out, go to sleep or the Iron Sheik will send you deep…".

The Iron Sheik will send you deep

But despite the outlandish stories that may be circulating, many seek my insight. I do travel around the world to be available to those who seek me, I have made it clear that those who understand these words do not need to meet me, those who do not understand these words have no reason to meet me and those who need to meet me will have no need to read these words. This leaves a very small group of individuals, so I have broadened the category slightly to include lonely but beautiful women with poor eyesight and damaged olfactory nerves and any person who is looking to lesson the burden of wealth in their lives. I could use a personal secretary was well, preferably one who fits into both of the prior categories.

But let me refocus, and quote from the profound philosopher A.E. Walinbrucke in his work *Verum Nihilim* nearly five centuries ago (translated from its original Latin):

> When we inquire into the apocalyptic apprehension that burdens the human consciousness, we are really looking at the fear that occurs when we construct our collective reality out of building blocks of time, belief and selfhood.
>
> Satan is cast down and sealed up for a thousand years in the Book of Revelations, which says that

Satan will be released for the final battle on a date certain. When shall we begin counting the thousand years? We must believe in those scriptures and the few who can interpret them in order to generate millennial fervor, and, of course, we must believe in our eternal soul to be concerned with its salvation when the end times come. More basically, we must be able to count, to conceptualize numbers and to understand these numbers in relationship to a common calendar overlay of our collective lives, the creation of a time based consensus reality. All of this is necessary to even have the idea that there could be an event of a thousand year cycle and it was not long ago that only a few of us could even count, let alone read.

The end of the world requires us to entertain an elaborate set of beliefs-as-actual and this has become easy for us to do since we are well practiced in the art of believing. We have been so well trained to believe without direct perception that we have even come to believe that we exist as discrete individuals, despite the fact that this belief brings with it untold conflict and pain. This conditioned sense of individuality colors all experience so thoroughly that we happily point to these experiences as the proof that we are indeed existent.

> With our selfhood intact, we now have a purpose in life, which is simply to survive.
>
> Just one issue challenges this robust self-referential reality—the self is entirely imaginary. That crack in the tautology is what we call fear, the knowing despite the conditioning that we are not independently existent and only life itself is without dependency on thought. When we push that challenge away, we simultaneously create the dualism of time and the end of time, we create the dichotomy of the world and the end of the world. When we accept the challenge to our reality, that our self is not actual but imagined, we allow the fear of the end to become the end of fear. The end of fear is the end of time is the end of the self and thankfully so.

What a brilliant philosopher he is, don't you agree! But, despite what Walinbrucke says, we don't go so easily. It is like the impoverished laborer who carries bags of cement day after day of his dreary, pointless life, when finally he throws down the sack he is carrying and calls out, "This life is too much, Death come and take me!" The Angel of Death arrives and says, "Man, why have you called me?!?" The man considers for a moment and says, "Uh, could you help me get this sack up on my back?" It may not be much of life that I am living but it is a life, and I still get to be at the center of it, so for the most part that trumps not living at all where I am not the center of anything. One could contemplate a life in which I live but where I am not the center of it, and this does suggest an interesting possibility, but few seem to be interested in it, after all, what is in it for me?

When I first discovered Walinbrucke's books, which are unfortunately quite rare now, I was at the Yale library and just by chance came upon them. I couldn't get enough of his ideas, I tore into the ancient work and devoured the very words on the pages therein, ravenous as I was for just a taste, and I was stopped only by the campus police who pulled the shredded remains of the books from my mouth before escorting me off campus. I believe that they have tightened security in their rare books area since that incident, no doubt to keep ruffians in uniforms from attacking a true bibliophile.

But, I digress…and while I am off on a tangent, let me go off on a tangent from that tangent and discuss the very real problem of taphephobia, which has been my constant companion since my realization that I was not. Any discussion of end-of-the-worldism would be incomplete without at least mentioning this fear of being buried alive. This phobia of mine was first triggered many years ago while I was discoursing on the empty nature of the self in Dewitt Park, across from the Samahara Bakery in Ithaca, New York. As I finished describing the emptiness of what is and the fullness of what is not to a small group of bemused passersby, I merged with that which is not and as with all the great ones, the eyes rolled up and catatonia set in as my world ended. Sweet enlightenment beyond even the thousand petaled lotus. Those who were there interpreted my absence as death, and amused as I was by the play of lila, I could not really disagree with them either philosophically, since I was not, or functionally, as I was entirely inert. Even after the coroner's people arrived and zipped me up in a body bag, I couldn't really object, it seemed fine enough, after all the bag they put me in was dark, moist and warm, a primal womb like the birth canal of the cosmic mother. This, as you might have guessed, triggered a profound rebirthing experience, bringing me out of totality and into the unintegrated trauma of my childhood as the bastard son of Franz Kafka and Alice B. Toklas, a son no one wanted and whose very existence was denied. I felt that I must push out with my head, pushing out of the groaning loins no longer of the cosmic mother, but of my actual mother, Alice B. Toklas, she trying to stop me, to deny me, to demonstrate to Gertrude that I was not the product of her and Kafka's singular dalliance, if she could keep me from coming out of her body then Momma Alice could show Gertrude that Nosirrah was not, that life could go on as usual in the Paris apartment and a rose could still be a rose could be a rose or whatever damn flower they wanted it to be. I fought to come into the light, to be born into the world of materiality, to inhale deeply the illusion of separation. My mother fought to keep me back, I pushed, she screamed, I pushed, and pushed, rebirthing with all my might, reaching deeply into the pain, letting out an ear splitting primal scream as I emerged into the light. I screamed and screamed. My eyes opened. I saw the bright light of the coroner's autopsy room where I sat up on the operating table, not a baby at all, just Nosirrah, my legs still held by the body bag. I felt cleansed, I felt good, much better than the assistant coroner who lay on the floor having heart palpitations from my little rebirthing screams, with the little cutting saw still whirring in his hand. I guess he thought I was dead.

And that is my point, tangential to the second degree as it may be. Just because I am not does not mean that I do not live. When the self dissolves into all that there is, then all that there is lives fully. Do not bury what is alive, and yes, dear reader, this is a beautifully constructed metaphor for each of our lives when we bury the truth and beauty of what we are in the conditioned construction of what we are not. But, my words are also to be taken literally, please do not bury me, even if I am not moving or breathing, unless you are quite certain about the situation. How will you know with certainty, you may ask. You will know only by giving up all of your ideas and opinions, all the accumulated knowledge of your lifetime, all the history of hurts and losses, all your hopes and dreams. You will know by entering with me into the space between thoughts, and there where you and I are not, you will certainly see what is and hence what is fully and totally alive. This is the end of the world of the personal self and it is a world few will give up, hence you can better understand my fear of being buried alive by those who know best but who know nothing at all about the universal energy we call life.

We do tend to love our personal world of our ideas, the world in which we exist and from which we attempt to communicate to others who inhabit their personal worlds of their ideas. It is not that different than an alien landing here and attempting to speak to an earthling, or me landing on Pluto to talk to Plutonians. Which really makes my point, since for me Pluto is a substantial planet worthy of inhabitation, but for the current crop of astronomers Pluto is now categorized as a minor dwarf planet along with Nix and Hydra (Nix and Hydra! These are not worthy to be spoken of in the same sentence as Pluto and I have asked my editor Lydia to remove them from the prior sentence, so if you notice that sentence ends abruptly, this is why, thank you, Lydia, for honoring my literary wishes). They say Pluto is just a chunk of ice and rock, part of the Kuiper Belt, just one of many Kuiper Belt Objects, a kind of floating debris field filled with left-over pieces from the formation of the solar system. What planet are these astronomers on?

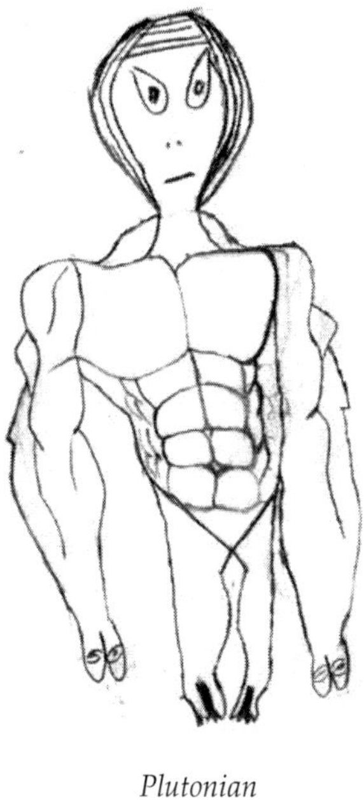

Plutonian

In my universe, Pluto is the last planet in the solar system on the chart in the classroom of Mrs. Neuswanger, who happened to be my beloved third grade teacher. She said it was a planet and so I say it is a planet and it is worthy of my landing there and meeting with the Plutonians and I couldn't very well meet with the Kuiper Belt Objectians. I am quite sure that the Plutonians would be horrified that these fresh-out-of-astronomy-school astronomers don't know all of this, which even a third grader knows. You see, while I know my world is made up of my beliefs, I also know that my beliefs are true and the reason I know that is because I learned everything I believe from somebody who knew what they were talking about, plus my beliefs make me feel safe and secure and I don't want to face the end of my world so I don't want to face the end of my beliefs. So you really have a choice here, you can agree with me and be part of my world or you can join the group of fools, apostates and lunatics who believe something entirely different and to whom I really do not have much to say, not that they would listen or, dare I express it, not that they would understand me with their weakened intellect, debauched morality, and generally unattractive features. I would prefer spending my time with a Plutonian, who, while technically not in my world, is certainly in my solar system, than I would with the disagreeable sorts who do not co-exist in my world, my solar system or even in my universe. This means that I am generally spending my free time conversing with Plutonians (they can transmit their thoughts inside our heads all the way from Pluto!) but I am still looking for someone, even one person, who shares my world. I haven't found anyone yet but I do have 6234 friends on my Facebook page, I just checked it, make that 6235, so even thought I don't really have any contact with any actual live person, between the Plutonians and my Facebook friends, I do have a full social life, at least in my imagination.

Hold on a another second, I have to do my Twitter tweet, I try to keep up on my life by tweeting what I am doing and I try to be totally honest and totally descriptive of the current moment when I am tweeting. I have tweeted thousands of times now but it is getting repetitive because there are only so many ways you can say "In this moment I am now tweeting…" but since that is all that is happening when I am tweeting having taken extensive Zen training to "walk when you are walking, eat when you are eating, and tweet when you are tweeting, you twit" then there is not much else I can say, which leaves quite a bit of the 140 characters unused. I am thinking of selling the remainder of the characters to corporate sponsors who can "advertise when you are advertising, pillage the Earth when you are pillaging".

All of this Facebook and Twitter referencing is to just indicate that Nosirrah may be slightly over the hill, or some might say decrepit, but Nosirrah is very contemporary in his outlook, he is, in the current vernacular of the street, very cool. I have been thinking about getting a mobile phone, but I don't understand, if someone wants to call you how do they know where you are? Maybe the phone has a really long cord. It would certainly take care of my aforementioned fear of being buried alive to be able to make a call from anywhere, although I wonder how the reception would be with six feet of dirt on top of me. I know that being able to get a call has something to do with the number of bars, which is no doubt why they call it a cell phone. Speaking of bars, a rabbi, a priest and Nosirrah walked into a bar, and the bartender said, "Nosirrah, what are you doing in this joke?" I had walked into the wrong bar, so I left just as the minister walked in.

I went down the street where I saw another bar, but I didn't walk into it, this time I ducked. At least I was in the right joke, even though it was a bad one.

I went further down the street where I walked into a psychiatrist's office.

"Doc," I said, patting myself on the back, "Without Nosirrah here, I would have gone crazy years ago."

"But you *are* Nosirrah!" the Doctor said, apparently not getting the joke, so I got serious. I told him that I am not, therefore Nosirrah is not, so the psychiatrist could not be correct that I was Nosirrah.

"I thought this was a psychiatrist joke, not some heavy philosophical spiel," the psychiatrist said.

Now he wants to laugh, so I thought about an interesting book I once came across in a chai shop in India with the odd but intriguing title *Doing Nothing,* which turned out to be a minimalist masterpiece that I would recommend you read as a life changing book if it did not create a conflict of interest to do so, and I did get to meet the author, despite his disinterest in being met by me, and who is everything I am not, but that is a story for another time, and to the point, this wonderful found book not only contained a heavy philosophical spiel but also had a psychiatrist joke about a man and a chicken and I couldn't remember it exactly but I did think of another version to tell the irritated psychiatrist from the prior paragraph to get us back to something remotely similar to a joke and I said, "OK, Doc, it is my sister, she thinks she is a chicken!"

"Well, why haven't you brought her in for treatment?" the psychiatrist said.

And I replied,"Well, we need the eggs."

With that I decided it was time to leave the jokes behind lest this otherwise respectable work become bogged down and I bid the psychiatrist,"Good day."

"What do you mean by good?" he asked, but I ignored him and he vanished into the wispy ethers of my mind, Nosirrah's mind, because despite the back and forth with the doctor, Nosirrah and I and all things, including authors who do not want to be met, are one, this One has no other, and therefore is not. And that is far too serious to be taken seriously.

I have wandered far from the topic of the end of the world, but that is quite intentional and clever as it shows us just how easily we are distracted by the mundane, how our life is overrun with the to do list, the errands, the relationship squabbles and the petty dramas of a day to day life. We barely notice that there is no guarantee that the next breath is going to occur, that our world could end just now, or for that matter, the world itself could end. And here we can see the tension that we manage each moment, between the prosaic and the passionate, the banal and the beautiful, the humdrum and the conundrum of existence itself. When we come to that fork in the road, we take the known even as we crave the unknown, we go for safety over and over, and wonder why we feel like life is a treadmill with scenery so repetitive that it might as well be patterns on the wallpaper.

But even so, even as we go once more for security, there is no guarantee of another breath. We are on the edge of the end and the edge of the end is the beginning. We push back from the edge and create the mundane as evidence of existence itself. The average and normal life that we manifest is a magnificent and beautiful dance at the border with oblivion. The mundane doesn't require the embellishment of specialness, of achievement, of out of the ordinary qualities, it is full in the fact of existence, it is incredibly textured, a dense flowering of qualities, in the face of non-existence.

Dearest, and I use this appellation to even those of you who are not speaking to me due to the fact that the small loans you have made to me over the years have not yet been paid back or you discovered your refrigerator quite a bit more empty after my last visit, yes, Dearest, your life, as it is, without one wit of change or improvement, is the exact expression of the universe coming into being out of nothing at all. You do not need to understand your actions, or judge your life, nor be wise, or good, or anything else that you have been told to do or to be. You are pure beauty without compare, love without an object, one without a second. You do not need to fear the end, but there is no real problem if you do. There is nothing for you to do but to be, and in that being to act, and in that action to love, and in that love to fill the void with energy so universal that existence and non-existence merge as mere aspects of each other, indivisible, undifferentiated and whole. Your life is the expression of endless possibilities, a quantum reality of unfathomable potential, creating without antecedent and expressing the vastness of totality in the singularity of this being who is not, but who is, a normal person living an everyday life whose world has ended and whose world is just created. There is nothing normal about normal when the world ends and when you see that with this moment passing as it is into nothing, that the world has indeed ended, then you have found freedom from all that you fear, for what can you fear when there is nothing at all?

Yes, there is something there in the nothing, not a thing, but an action, a movement, the unfolding mystery of creation.

This is the beginning of the end of this book, a book written backwards, not about the end of the world as it may have seemed in the beginning, but about the beginning of the world as it may now be evident, and life itself, as in this book, where the end is the beginning, the beginning cannot be adequately described, or even known, as it is entirely fresh and without the burden of what was before or what will be. The beginning is creation itself without anything to condition it and where there is the beginning the words will have stopped and not yet begun again, stillness that is a full, dynamic movement.

And this is just the beginning.

Sentient Publications, LLC publishes books on cultural creativity, experimental education, transformative spirituality, holistic health, new science, ecology, and other topics, approached from an integral viewpoint. Our authors are intensely interested in exploring the nature of life from fresh perspectives, addressing life's great questions, and fostering the full expression of the human potential. Sentient Publications' books arise from the spirit of inquiry and the richness of the inherent dialogue between writer and reader.

Our Culture Tools series is designed to give social catalyzers and cultural entrepreneurs the essential information, technology, and inspiration to forge a sustainable, creative, and compassionate world.

We are very interested in hearing from our readers. To direct suggestions or comments to us, or to be added to our mailing list, please contact:

SENTIENT PUBLICATIONS, LLC
1113 Spruce Street
Boulder, CO 80302
303-443-2188
contact@sentientpublications.com
www.sentientpublications.com